"Miss Cresswell," said Officer Leeman,

"I called your license into our computer bank—
purely routine, you understand. But I'm afraid
you'll have to come with me to headquarters.
Your friend can follow along in your car."

"Am I being cited for the accident?" Emma
asked.

"No, ma'am," said the policeman. "We're putting that down to hazardous driving conditions."

Emma was cold and tired and she just wanted
to get to a hotel. "So what is the problem, then?"

"The problem," Officer Leeman said, "is that
you are listed as a missing person."

The Sunset Island series
by Cherie Bennett

Sunset Island
Sunset Kiss
Sunset Dreams
Sunset Farewell
Sunset Reunion
Sunset Secrets

Sunset Secrets

Cherie Bennett

SPLASH™

A BERKLEY / SPLASH BOOK

SUNSET SECRETS is an original publication
of The Berkley Publishing Group.
This work has never appeared before in book form.

SUNSET SECRETS

A Berkley Book / published by arrangement with
General Licensing Company, Inc.

PRINTING HISTORY
Berkley edition / April 1992

A GLC BOOK

Splash is a trademark of General Licensing Company, Inc.

ISBN: 0-425-13319-2

A BERKLEY BOOK ® TM 757,375
Berkley Books are published by The Berkley Publishing Group,
200 Madison Avenue, New York, New York 10016.
The name "BERKLEY" and the "B" logo
are trademarks belonging to Berkley Publishing Corporation.

PRINTED IN THE UNITED STATES OF AMERICA

10 9 8 7 6 5 4 3 2 1

For Jeff

ONE

"I am about to fall madly in love," Sam Bridges announced meaningfully over the phone to her two best friends, Emma Cresswell and Carrie Alden.

"Who?" Emma asked with surprise.

"Yeah, who?" Carrie echoed.

It was a natural question. The last time the three of them had been together was Christmas vacation, three months earlier. Emma, Sam, and Carrie had taken a trip to Miami. And although Sam had had an *almost* serious encounter with a hot young rock star, to Emma and Carrie's knowledge all that was in the past. So who had Sam met, they wondered, that she hadn't even mentioned in all their long-distance conference calls between Towson, Maryland (where Emma was a freshman at elite Goucher College), Orlando, Florida (where Sam was a dancer at Disney World), and New Haven, Connecticut (where Carrie was a freshman at Yale)?

"Is it Goofy?" Carrie asked, referring to Sam's

friend Danny Franklin, who played Goofy at Disney World.

"Hey, he may be Goofy, but he's my Goofy," Sam quipped. "Anyway, it isn't Danny. Goofy and I are, as the saying goes, just friends," she said.

"So who then?" Emma asked.

"Details are not important," Sam replied breezily. "It's the intent that counts."

"Yes, but who is the intended?" Carrie pressed.

"I don't exactly know," Sam admitted, "but that's the best part!"

"I think the translation of that is that she isn't exactly seeing anyone," Emma told Carrie with a laugh.

"Hey, that only applies to right now," Sam pointed out. "I could meet the guy of my dreams during the Rockin' Fifties Revue this afternoon. He could be watching me from the front row, thinking I'm the most gorgeous and talented babe he's ever seen. We'd make eye contact right before I go into my cartwheel. Fifteen minutes later we could be swapping spit right under Mickey and Minnie's noses."

"As long as it's not Goofy's nose," Carrie said. "I have a feeling he'd like to be much more to you than just a friend."

"No, Danny's okay about it," Sam said. "He'd be happy to shake hands with my Romeo Man."

"Romeo Man?" Emma laughed.

"I like to throw in the occasional quaint expression," Sam said.

"Oh, it's quaint, all right," Carrie agreed.

2

"Hey, my motto is, live on the edge of possibility," Sam decreed blithely. "Knowing Mr. Tall, Dark, and Rich could walk into my life at any moment sort of keeps me going through my ten zillionth high kick at the Wonderful World of Disney. Sometimes I don't think I can stand it another millisecond," Sam said.

"It was your choice," Carrie pointed out. "You're the one who wanted to drop out of college to take a job dancing there."

"Right," Emma agreed. "You could quit if you wanted to, and go back to school."

"Pardonnez-moi, but some of us have to work to pay the bills," Sam told Emma huffily, "though I realize this is not a concept to which you can relate."

Emma's money was a sore point with Sam, and sometimes Sam pounced on Emma's most innocent remarks. Emma was rich. Sam was not. Actually, different as all three of them were in background and personality, it still amazed them that they had become friends at all, much less best friends.

Emma was a Cresswell of the Boston Cresswells, one of the wealthiest families in the country. She had never had to do a day of work in her life. In fact, she'd shocked her parents the summer before, when she'd taken a job as an au pair on Sunset Island. Emma had been educated in Europe, spoke five languages, and was on a first-name basis with royalty. She longed to escape from the hypocritical, narrow confines of

3

the life prescribed for her—maybe even to join the Peace Corps one day—but so far she hadn't been able to get up the nerve to confront her overbearing mother with her decision. Instead she just continued along as a French major at her mother's alma mater, snooty Goucher College, trying to decide what she really wanted to do and hoping that she hadn't been a pampered rich girl for so long that she no longer had what it would take to follow through with her dreams.

Carrie Alden came from an upper-middle-class family in New Jersey, where both her parents were pediatricians. Level-headed Carrie, who had always been an excellent student, was thrilled to be at Yale studying photography. If anything, Carrie tended to be too perfect, trying too hard to be everything to everyone.

And then there was Sam—irrepressible, one-of-a-kind Samantha Bridges. Much to Sam's chagrin, up until a few months ago she had lived her entire life in the tiny town of Junction, Kansas. It was home, she said, to a few cows and acres and acres of cornfields. A few weeks after starting college on a dance scholarship at Kansas State, Sam had auditioned for a job dancing at Disney World. She'd gotten it and had dropped out of college without even telling her parents. Of course they had had a fit when they found out. But Sam felt certain that college was not for her, and dancing at Disney World was just a step to bigger and better things. She aspired to fame and fortune, with the emphasis on fortune. How she

4

would achieve it, she didn't know. All she knew was that she wished she could be there already.

"Hey, I thought this phone call was to talk about the party," Carrie reminded them, smoothly changing subjects. She was used to being a buffer between Sam and Emma.

"It's going to be fabulous, incredible, and outrageous," Sam enthused, already forgetting her momentary pique with Emma. "It is so nice of Graham and Claudia to offer their house for a spring-break bash."

"I agree," Emma said, willing to forget Sam's barbed comment. "Can you believe it's been over seven months since we were on Sunset Island?"

Sunset Island was where the three girls had become best friends the previous summer, and it was to Sunset Island they were about to return over spring break for the party of the year.

All three of them thought back to the past spring, when they had met at the National Au Pair Society convention in New York City. They'd come to like one another during the three days of classes and interviews, and had been really happy to find out they'd all been hired to work for the summer on fabulous Sunset Island, a resort island off the coast of Maine. Each girl had lived with the family that hired her, taking care of their kids and being a general helper, in return for room, and board, and a small salary. The best part was that Sunset Island was famous not only for its spectacular beaches and breathtaking sunsets, but for its parties with the rich, wild, and sometimes famous. All three girls had been ready for a summer of adventure before the realities of college took over their lives, and all three of them had found it.

"What you mean, Emma, is can we believe that it's been over seven months since you've seen Kurt?" Carrie teased.

The Kurt Carrie referred to was Kurt Ackerman, the first guy Emma had ever fallen in love with. Kurt had grown up on Sunset Island, and Emma had met him when she'd taken her three-year-old charge, Katie, for swimming lessons at the Sunset Country Club. Kurt was the head swimming instructor. Between that summer job and driving a taxi at night, he was putting himself through college at the University of Maine. Emma and Kurt had vowed that her being rich and his being poor wouldn't affect their relationship, but it had anyway. There had been so many misunderstandings and recriminations that Emma had finally broken up with Kurt at the end of the summer. The final straw had come when Kurt had started dating Emma's worst enemy, Diana De Witt. Their relationship had *not* been platonic. Emma had felt as if she'd been stabbed in the back—she didn't feel that she could ever trust Kurt again.

And yet she couldn't seem to change what was in her heart. She knew she'd made mistakes, too, and perhaps they both had rushed into a relationship they weren't really ready for. After a couple of months, Emma had written a letter to Kurt, but Kurt had never answered it. Then, just when Emma had begun to tell herself she had to give up on Kurt, even if it broke her heart, she'd received a long, heartfelt response. Emma's tears had fallen on the pages as she read that Kurt, too, couldn't stop thinking about her, that he still loved her, that the only reason he hadn't answered sooner was that it was so important to him to get down on paper exactly how he felt. He'd said he was scared, but more than anything else he wanted a second chance. Emma had written back that she felt the same way, that they both would learn from their mistakes of the summer. Now that the girls were planning this reunion party, Emma would soon see Kurt again. Just the thought of being with him again, of being wrapped in his arms, made Emma shiver all over. It definitely made concentrating on French literature difficult, if not impossible.

"I always told you the guy loves you," Sam said. "I'm really glad you're going to get back together."

"We're going to try, anyway," Emma said cautiously.

"Oh, please," Sam scoffed. "Five minutes after we hit Sunset Island you two will be in the dunes tearing off each other's clothes."

"Oh well, I guess that means I don't need to help plan this party, then, since I won't be there," Emma said with a laugh.

"Hey, this is a team effort, remember?" Sam reminded her.

7

"I know we decided to meet up before the party," Carrie said, "but we didn't decide where. How about if you guys come to Yale, and we hang out here, and then fly up to Sunset Island?"

"Sounds like fun," Emma said. "I love New Haven."

"And Yale guys are seriously cute," Carrie added.

"Forget seriously cute, let's talk about seriously rich," Sam remarked.

"Never fear, Sam," Carrie said with a laugh, "some of them are seriously both."

"In that case, I'm there!" Sam giggled.

"You won't have any trouble taking so much time off from your job?" Emma asked Sam.

"Like I told you last time you asked," Sam said, "they love me at Disney World. Besides, there are understudies who are just dying to get on the stage instead of watching from the wings, so not to worry."

"As long as you're absolutely sure—" Carrie began.

"Hey, you two," Sam interrupted, "I have a mother, so chill out."

"Speaking of mothers," Carrie said, "my mom came up to New Haven last week for a medical conference. I finally introduced her to Billy. The three of us went to a Garth Brooks concert."

Billy Sampson was one of the two guys Carrie was dating. He was the lead singer for Flirting with Danger (or the Flirts, as everyone called them), the hottest band in the Maine area. They

8

were even starting to get some national recognition. Billy and the rest of the guys in the band were renting an old house on Sunset Island, which was where Carrie had met him the previous summer. She'd been dating him ever since, but she still hadn't resolved her relationship with her longtime high school boyfriend, Josh, who was now going to school with her at Yale. Carrie thought she just wanted to be friends with Josh now, and he definitely wanted more. He went crazy every time Billy came to Yale to visit Carrie.

"You went to a concert with your mother and your boyfriend who sings rock and roll, has a ponytail, and has a pierced ear?" Sam asked. "My mother would have dragged me back to Junction so fast the tread marks would still be smoking on the highway."

Carrie laughed. "My mom was pretty cool about it," she told them, "although she did say that it was weird to see me with someone other than Josh. Anyhow, she loves Garth Brooks, so it was a great equalizer."

"Hey, I hate to break up the conversation, but I've got a one o'clock class and it's ten to one," Emma said.

"What's more important, your class or Carrie's love life?" Sam demanded.

"Carrie's love life, definitely," Emma said, "but unfortunately I don't get tested on that!"

"I gotta boogie, too," Sam said. "I have a rehearsal for a new dance number."

"And I suppose I should go to the library and do some research for my American history paper," Carrie said with a sigh.

After deciding that they'd hold their next conference call two days later at the same time, the girls hung up. Emma grabbed her books and headed from her expensive one-bedroom high-rise apartment toward campus. Carrie dialed Josh's dorm room to see if he wanted to go to the library with her. And Sam changed clothes—not into a leotard and tights, which is what she would normally wear to a rehearsal, but into black pants, a white shirt, and a black vest.

Sam sighed. She didn't really have a rehearsal for a new dance number at Disney World. One week earlier she had been fired. Now she was dressed in her uniform for her second day of work at Big Al's Steak House. Sam was a waitress now.

She just couldn't bear to admit it to her friends.

TWO

Life sucks. That's what Sam thought as she accidentally banged her long legs into the edge of one of the tables at Big Al's for what already seemed like the thousandth time. As she rubbed at the spot, which she knew would soon turn an ugly purple color just like the spot above it, tears came to her eyes. *How could this have happened to me?* Just days before, she had been a dancer at Disney World, dreaming of Vegas chorus lines, solos in Broadway shows, and grand entrances at Sardi's. Today she was a waitress on the dinner shift, serving tourists in polyester pantsuits. She was not, to be sure, a happy camper.

"Hey, waitress! I ordered a baked potato, not fries!" a Midwestern-accented voice called out.

"Dear, we asked for water ten minutes ago," an elderly woman said, tapping on Sam's arm as she raced by.

"Yo, girlie, can we talk menus here? My kid is starving."

Don't think, Sam counseled herself. *You will*

11

lose your mind if you think. She hurried around the restaurant, hitting her legs three more times, then burning her hand when she grabbed a heated plate too hastily.

"Sam, why don't you take your break?" the other waitress suggested in a kind voice. Callie McMartin had been a professional waitress for thirty years. She felt sorry for Sam, and secretly thought she wouldn't last in the business for thirty days.

"Thanks," Sam said gratefully, holding her burnt hand gingerly and heading for the kitchen area, where the employees ate.

Sam grabbed a burger and was about to ease her feet out of the clunky black rubber-soled shoes that Big Al forced the waiters and waitresses to wear (Big Al had gone ballistic when Sam came to work wearing her trademark red cowboy boots). She stared down at her aching feet, encased in the ugliest shoes ever created by man, and she just couldn't help it—tears swam in her eyes. She thought back to what was to date probably the stupidest thing she had ever done— the thing that had gotten her fired from her dancing job.

It came down to a personality conflict, Sam supposed, but she found it hard not to blame herself for the part her own strong will had played in what she now saw as a monumental career setback. Carrie and Emma had often objected to her egocentric tendencies, but they'd always forgiven her in the end. Now—hindsight is always 20/20, Sam realized—she could see that a difference of opinion was one thing between friends and quite another between a boss and an employee, or, in this case, a dancer and a director of choreography.

Not that Sam hadn't been duly impressed by Mr. Christopher at first. At the beginning, in the thrill of auditioning, then winning a place with the Disney World dance troupe, she'd taken the choreographer's directions as the word of God and felt like a favored angel in the bargain. Her long legs, supple five-foot-ten frame, flaming red hair, and what Mr. Christopher had called her "presence" had soon moved her from the back row to center stage in the lineup, and in the process had resulted in a few jealousies among the other dancers.

So what, she'd thought as she basked in her own glory. *I'm not here to worry about other people's sour grapes*. Now she wondered if the support of her peers might have changed anything.

But even when Sam had most admired him, Mr. Christopher had reminded her of a bug, specifically a June bug, one of those buzzing beetlelike creatures that assaulted screen doors under summer porch lights. For one, he was hyperactive and he scuttled—that was the only word for it. Bulbous, protruding eyes and a couple of stray hairs that had a way of standing up from his thinning crown when he was agitated (which was often) enhanced the image, which was completed by his choice of wardrobe: baggy pants and long, shapeless cardigan sweaters or jackets.

It hadn't taken long for Sam to figure out how Mr. Christopher had earned the nicknames that made their way through the dancers' dressing rooms. Though no one had made fun of his sexual orientation (he was unabashedly gay), his affectations ran from annoying to downright obnoxious. As Leonard, Sam's dance partner, had expressed it, "Gay is about sexual preference. It's not an excuse to be whiny, bitchy, or shrill—that only gives the rest of us a bad image." Mr. Christopher's voice tended toward a grating, petulant quality during rehearsals. His pet obsession was crispness.

"Puh-leez, Samantha! You're absolutely wilting on me! Keep it crisp! Crisp!"

"Are we in a dance revue or a salad spinner?" Sam had whispered to Leonard.

A few days later, someone had altered the sign pointing in the direction of the dressing rooms so it read "Salad Dressing Rooms." The other dancers could barely control their laughter, and Sam had felt she was finally a real member of the troupe. Now, looking back, it might have been the point at which, smartswise, she became a real vegetable. Buoyed by the confidence of feeling she belonged, it wasn't long before she was overstepping her bounds in a rehearsal for the Wild West Revue.

"And reach-two, reach-two, spin-two, dip-two, jump-two, splits . . . and hold!" barked the Critter—as in Crispy Critter—which was that

14

week's moniker for the choreography director. Everyone had held. Almost immediately the Critter had darted from the wings and scuttled across the stage. "Okay, everybody up, and places, please. Samantha, if you don't mind telling me, what, exactly, was that move there at the end? It certainly wasn't a split."

"Well, it's, um, just a little variation I worked out on my own time," Sam had said, not sounding nearly as assured as she'd meant to. It was true that the move, two rapid alternating waist-high kicks with both feet off the ground at once, had required hours of practice. She'd made sure she could do it flawlessly before springing it on the troupe and her director. She had hoped it would lead to more recognition, maybe even a solo. She had anticipated applause.

"Is it your opinion that this routine needs variation?" the Critter had asked innocently.

Might as well go for broke, she'd thought. "To be honest, it does seem like this is almost the exact same routine we do for the Rockin' Fifties Revue. I mean, except for a couple do-si-dos."

Someone in the back line had tittered. Emboldened, Sam had continued, "I thought the kicks might look more cowboy, you know, more rodeo, more Wild West. I'm not sure a cowgirl would even do splits. After all, they have cactuses and all kinds of prickly things on the ground out there—it could be painful."

The suppressed laughter had erupted then, but Mr. Christopher hadn't cracked a smile. His eyes had seemed to bulge out farther from their sockets as the last sounds died onstage.

"Thank you for that edifying lecture on the dance techniques of our western states," Mr. Christopher had said. "We're on a ten-minute break here. Samantha, I wonder if you'd be so kind as to grace my office with your presence."

Sam's heart had been thudding as she pushed open the door marked E. J. Christopher, Director of Choreography. She'd tried for her most dazzling smile, but it had frozen before it cleared her teeth when she saw her employment folder in the hands of the director.

"Come in, Samantha, and shut the door behind you."

"M-Mr. Crisp—I mean, Christopher, I'm really sorry if I disrupted rehearsal. It wasn't at all what I'd—"

"Don't waste my time or yours, Samantha. It wasn't really working out, anyway."

"Wasn't wor—what do you mean?"

"You're a stunning girl, as I'm sure you're aware, with a fiery personality to match that hair of yours. Unfortunately, individuality is not what we're after here."

Sam interjected, "I know, I know, and it won't happen again, I promise! I'll never be original again. I'll do everything you say, I really will! Now that I understand a little better . . ."

Mr. Christopher had stopped Sam's babble with a graceful hand held upright. For the first time she had seen something like kindness in his expression.

"My dear Samantha, I have a feeling the good Lord did not put you on this earth with the intent that you never be original. Frankly, you scream of originality. So perhaps it's my fault in thinking that this might have worked out."

"But it will!" Sam had interrupted. "I can—"

"No, you really can't," Mr. Christopher had said mildly. "I have a job to do and, if you will, a product to deliver. In some situations your standing out from the crowd would be an asset, but here it isn't. I realize you'll take this as a rejection, and I'm sorry about that. But it isn't fair to you, or to me, to put this off any longer. I'm terminating your contract as of today."

Sam had fled from his office in tears, too miserable even to try to retreat with dignity. She'd been grateful that neither of her roommates, two flight attendants, was home at their tiny, seedy excuse for an apartment. Even after almost six months, she hardly knew them. Usually they'd been either out of town or partying, and she'd always been rehearsing, performing, or partying herself. Now she didn't know where the next rent check was coming from, and she wasn't in the mood to discuss it with virtual strangers.

Sam hated being alone, though. She had desperately needed to talk with someone. Carrie and Emma had immediately come to mind. They were the only ones who would understand how absolutely tragic this was.

Or maybe not, she'd thought. She could just hear practical Carrie telling her that getting fired from Disney World wasn't exactly life-threatening. Carrie would probably bring up their narrow escape from death at sea during Christmas break.

Now *that* had been life-threatening. At a party on a yacht off the coast of Miami, the three of them had been cut adrift on a tiny dinghy, and were lost at sea during a torrential storm.

And when she'd thought about it, how could Emma possibly relate to some stupid little dancing job at Disney World, when all she had ever had to do in her life was look perfect and decide how to spend money?

No, Sam had decided, she really couldn't tell Carrie or Emma, much as she might like to. Their good opinion of her simply meant too much—she was not willing to risk losing it.

"Better put on your skates, girl. You just got a party of ten and they want separate checks." Big Al's voice dropped Sam rudely back into the here and now. *Yuck.*

"Be right there," Sam sighed, lacing up the loathsome black shoes.

Okay, she vowed as she double-knotted the left lace, *I can deal with this. I'll just pretend I'm an actress in a play, and this is only act one. By the end of the play I'll be a rich and incredibly famous dancer, and—*

Hey, wait a minute, Sam thought, stopping before she pushed through the swinging door into the dining room. *I'm on to something here. If I can pretend I'm an actress, why can't I be an actress? Actresses are original! I didn't get fired for being incompetent, after all. Dancing at Disney World is not the only game in town, thank you very much!*

As Sam filled the water glasses for her new table, her mind was buzzing. Orlando was currently booming as a center for the movie industry. It was a town full of opportunities for an original, talented vixen such as herself. And, hey, lots of famous actresses had had to wait tables in their climb to the top.

Sam straightened her shoulders as she carried her tray of water glasses to the table. A mirror on the wall caught her eye. There she was, in that drab waitress outfit, her glorious hair pulled back into a bun. *Truly a hideous sight.* Sam sighed and set the glasses on the table with a thud. A baby mushed his well-gummed cookie into her stomach and stared up at her with a toothless grin.

Yeah, right, Sam thought. *Like any producer is going to recognize my potential here at Big Al's Steak House.*

"Darling, you're not busy, are you?" came Emma's mother's voice through the phone.

Emma was, but she knew from experience it wouldn't do any good to tell that to Katerina Cresswell.

"Go ahead, Mother, I've got a few minutes."

"Lucky you. If I get tapped for one more charity ball committee, I'll be down to absolute

19

milliseconds of free time. As it is, I'm planning a retreat to Glen Echo next week, just to offset the stress."

Glen Echo was an exclusive Colorado spa for the mega-rich. Emma had once made the mistake of referring to it—within earshot of her mother—as pamper-therapy for gilded heifers, but her New Year's resolution was to try to be nicer to her mother, no matter what.

"That's nice, Mother. I'm sure the change of pace will do you good."

"You really must start calling me Kat, Emma," her mother said. "You know no one believes I'm old enough to have a daughter your age—wouldn't it be much nicer?"

This was one request that Emma just couldn't bring herself to honor, New Year's resolution or no New Year's resolution, so she just kept her mouth shut.

"I know you'll try to remember about the name thing," Kat supplied. "By the way, have you heard from your father lately?"

Neat segue, Emma thought. Katerina Cresswell always did manage to get around to her point quickly, single-minded as she was about her every desire. So her mother wanted to talk to Emma about her father. That was the real reason she had called. Emma should have known her mother wouldn't call for permission to take a vacation.

Emma sighed and rubbed her temples, which began to throb whenever one of her parents wanted to talk with her about the other. Her parents had been negotiating—if you could call it that—a very sticky divorce for what seemed like a lifetime. At this point they talked only through their respective lawyers, except in the instances when one or the other tried to pull information out of Emma. Another of her resolutions had been to stay as far as she could get from the front line of their battles. They hadn't ever been a real family, and lately not even a pretend family. Emma figured it was simply none of her business anymore.

"Somehow, Mother," she replied, "I suspect that you know very well I haven't heard from Dad." Resolution *numero uno* was starting to falter.

"What about the great mystery of your Christmas present?"

Emma's father had been dropping hints since Christmas about a special present, that would be awaiting her on her next visit. Emma hadn't seen her father for the holidays, even though she'd been as close as a cab ride. He was in Palm Beach with his new girlfriend, Valerie, who was (much to Emma's embarrassment) only a few years older than Emma herself. Had Emma stayed in Florida, as she'd planned, she might have gotten up the nerve to storm the fortress of that little love nest. But the Florida vacation had ended early when Carrie and Sam had decided they wanted to be home for part of the Christmas season after all, and Emma had ended up going back to Boston.

Not that there had been anything to go back to except her lonely apartment. Sure, there was the family mansion on Beacon Hill, but Emma's mother was so involved with trying desperately to hold on to her love affair with twenty-five-year-old artist Austin Payne that she had barely paid any attention to Emma.

"Emma? Are you there?" Kat trilled into the phone.

"I'm here, Mother," Emma sighed, burrowing down into her plush white-on-white jacquard velvet chair.

"Didn't your father's Christmas telegram say he had a big surprise for you in the new year?"

Emma sat up quickly. "And just how do you happen to know that?"

"I'm redecorating, dear," Kat said smoothly. "You left it out in your bedroom in plain sight at Christmastime."

"It was in the drawer of my nightstand," Emma snapped. Her hand gripped the phone receiver and her knuckles turned white. This was going too far, even for her mother.

"Emma, I certainly have to clean things out before I can redecorate," Kat explained self-righteously.

"Mother," Emma began, "you've never cleaned out anything in your life except maybe a bank account."

"And how fortunate for me that there's always

more money to fill it right up again!" Kat answered gaily.

Emma sighed again. Her head was really beginning to throb now. "Listen, Mother, I have to go. I have an exam in Renaissance history to study for."

"Oh, well, if you can't spare the time for me, I understand," Kat said, switching to her little-girl voice.

"It's just that I have to get to the library—"

"Just remember that I'm the one who called you, Emma, not your father, that's all I ask. That's fair, isn't it?"

"What are you talking about?" Emma said, completely confused.

"If anyone should ever ask you which parent cares enough to call . . ." Kat began.

"Anyone who?" Emma demanded. Her irritation was now definitely greater than any resolution. Oh, her mother drove her *crazy!*

"Anyone like, oh, a lawyer or someone," Kat continued innocently. "One never knows."

"Fine," Emma said. *Anything to end this conversation!*

"I'll just toddle off now, dear," Kat sang. "Be sure to get your beauty sleep. Remember, college comes to an end, but crow's-feet last forever!"

Emma had barely hung up when the phone rang again.

"Hi, sweetheart. How's Daddy's princess?"

Great, thought Emma, *a double-header*. Still, she couldn't seem to have quite the same animosity toward her father that she did toward her mother. She always felt as if he really wanted to be close to her, but just didn't seem to know how to do it.

"Hi, Dad. What's up?" Emma asked, settling back into the plush chair cushions.

"I was about to ask you the same thing. How's school?"

"Fine," Emma answered.

"You enjoy it, princess," her father said. "College was a wonderful time in my life, you know."

"I know, Daddy," she said gently. Although Emma's father was one of the most successful multimillionaires in the country, he often seemed to long for his college days. Emma guessed that everything had seemed simpler to him back then— no board meetings, none of the pressure of running the family businesses, no Katerina.

"So, listen, princess," her father continued. "What's the world coming to when a young girl can hold out till March without even asking about her Christmas present?"

"Oh well, you know . . ." Emma began lamely, twisting the phone cord around her fingers. How could she explain that her father's presence would have meant much more to her than any gift he might dream up? But she was too old to go begging for affection like some little kid. It was too late for all that, anyway.

"The point of my call is that I think you've waited long enough," her father's voice boomed through the phone. "How soon can you get down here?"

"To Palm Beach?" Emma asked, confused. "I wasn't planning to come to—"

"Be spontaneous!" her father interrupted. "Spring break is coming up. What better time to head for Florida?"

Emma didn't mention that she'd just been in Florida a few months ago. "Actually, Daddy, I've already made plans for spring break."

"So how about you come to Palm Beach before wherever it is that you're headed?" her father suggested.

"Gee, Daddy, I don't think—"

"Wouldn't spring break be a lot more fun in a snappy new convertible?" her father coaxed her.

"You're buying me a new car?"

"You pick it out, it's yours!" Her father's voice boomed eagerly through the phone. "I've been waiting so you could pick it out yourself. Wouldn't that be great?"

"That's really nice of you, Daddy, but—"

"And while you're here," her father continued, "you could finally meet Valerie."

Valerie. Her father's girlfriend. Fiancée. Whatever. Meeting her was not exactly Emma's idea of a good time. And meeting Valerie was obviously the true purpose of her father's invitation to Palm Beach. Emma definitely needed time to figure out what she was going to do.

Emma leaned forward. "Listen, Dad, I'm expecting a call from my tutor, and it's really important. See, I was sick and missed some classes, and there's a test tomorrow." She paused. "I'll think about how I could work that out and get back to you, okay?"

When her dad had hung up, Emma turned the ringer off and set the answering machine to pick up. The headache that had begun with her mother's phone call was now pounding mercilessly through her skull. Her stomach was tied in knots; even her hands were shaking. How could she let her parents affect her this way? She vowed over and over that she'd be cool, that she wouldn't let them meddle in her life or hurt her anymore. But somehow she always found herself somewhere in the middle, with this horrible headache that cut like a knife.

Lately, only one thing seemed to help a little, and that was a glass of wine. At least it eased the worst of the tension until she could begin to think of what to do.

Emma padded into the kitchen and took a bottle of white wine out of the refrigerator. She'd been keeping a few bottles of good wine on hand in case she had company. Then she'd discovered that even at snooty Goucher College most of the kids drank beer, not wine. Besides, she hadn't really met anyone she wanted to have over, anyway.

She had, however, gone through two of the bottles of wine already. Lately she'd been treating herself to a glass of wine at bedtime. It helped her relax and fall asleep, and took her mind off the hodgepodge of questions that seemed to creep in whenever she let down her guard: Kurt, the Peace Corps, school, and most of all the constant tension in her family. Frankly, all of it made her sick sometimes.

Emma opened a bottle of chardonnay she'd been saving for a special occasion, poured a glass, and took it with her to change for bed. After slipping into her favorite Chinese silk pajamas, Emma walked back over the lush oyster-shell-colored carpet to the living room, where she flicked on her favorite classical station. She savored the wine. *This is definitely helping to clear my thoughts*, she said to herself.

She now considered her father's offer from a new perspective. Wouldn't spring break on Sunset Island and a romantic rendezvous with Kurt be improved by a snappy new convertible? At the height of the previous summer's relationship, Emma would have said that Kurt was way too down to earth to be impressed by something as superficial as a new car. Then Diana De Witt had whisked him off to New York for a dream weekend on her bankroll, and Emma had learned a bitter truth: even people who insist they aren't influenced by money can fall prey to the lure of the almighty dollar.

Of course, if Kurt was still enthralled by that kind of display, Emma really didn't want him. Still, it might not hurt to make a good impression. Though she'd dated a few different guys since she'd begun college, no one could compare to Kurt. Just the thought of his blue eyes and the memory of his arms around her made her feel that her heart was still imprisoned by the magic of the previous summer.

But it was a scary way to feel. It made her feel too vulnerable. And no matter what Kurt's letter said, there was always the possibility that she cared about him more than he cared about her. So if she showed up in an incredibly hot new car, just maybe it would make it seem that her life without him was more exciting than it really had been.

Surprised to see that she'd just about finished her wine, Emma went to the refrigerator for a touch more. She had pulled the cork and was lifting the bottle when she recalled hearing—or had she read it somewhere?—that drinking alone was a warning sign of alcoholism. *Ridiculous*, she thought, *I hardly drink at all!* Still, she was careful to fill the glass only halfway this time.

Her parents had never thought twice about ordering her a glass of wine at any of their fancy restaurants or resorts. And certainly it had been available at all of the parties they had attended. Screwed up as her mother and father were, Emma reflected, they were not alcoholics. When Emma's childhood companion Trent Hayden-Bishop, had deemed to make up for the trouble he had caused her on Sunset Island the summer before, sending her a very convincing ID stating her age as twenty-one, Emma hadn't hesitated to slip it into the inner pocket of her wallet. The fact was, people were generally impressed by her poise and obvious wealth, and assumed she was of legal drinking age anyway. They rarely asked her for identification.

Savoring each sip (she'd have to remember this vintage, it really was good), she settled back on the couch to think through her travel plans. She could always make a very, very short visit to her father, pick out a car, then scoop up Sam on the way north through Orlando. Wouldn't Sam just love a road trip in a brand-new, to-die-for convertible?

The thought of looking cool, rich, and carefree in Sam's eyes pleased Emma somehow. Sam was so good at grabbing the reins of her life and galloping ahead. Emma had to admit she envied her for that.

Suddenly she couldn't wait for the scheduled conference call with her friends. She was going to take up her dear daddy's offer, and she was going to plan the entire trip!

Emma took one more sip, set her wineglass carefully on one of the hand-woven coasters she'd bought to protect her new mahogany coffee table, and reached for the phone.

THREE

"It's confession time, Ms. Goody Two Shoes!"

It was early the next morning, and Emma's voice was teasing over the phone, but Carrie felt like her brain wouldn't kick in until she'd had a shower and two or three cups of coffee.

"Huh?" was her sterling response.

"I must have left you four messages last night!" Emma cried, "then I finally gave up somewhere past the witching hour. So was it Josh, or Billy, or someone new?"

Carrie cleared her throat and wiped her eyes blearily with the back of her hand. "As a matter of fact, I was in the darkroom until seven, the library until it closed at eleven, and downstairs in the study room until almost two."

"Yale's tough, huh?" Emma said compassionately.

"Nothing I can't handle," Carrie assured her. "So what were these frantic phone calls about?"

"A great idea I wanted to run by you and Sam," Emma said eagerly. "I finally found Sam after eleven. I was bursting by that time!"

"So what is it?" Carrie asked.

"Could I interest you in a plan that would take us to Sunset Island in high style?"

"Sure," ventured Carrie, "let's hear it."

Quickly Emma filled Carrie in on her conversation with her father. She'd planned on asking for some words of wisdom about her mother's call, too—Carrie was so level-headed—but Emma decided that with Carrie working so hard at school, it really wasn't fair to ask for free mental-health counseling.

"A new car!" Carrie cried. "That's great! You mean you're going to drive it to Sunset Island?"

"We're *all* taking it to Sunset Island—that is, if you guys agree," Emma answered. "Here's the plan. First I'll fly to Palm Beach and pick up the car, then I'll drive to Orlando and get Sam."

"You mean you'll pick up the car and meet Valerie," Carrie corrected Emma. "You left out that detail." Emma had told Carrie about her father's girlfriend months earlier, and Carrie knew that the last thing Emma wanted to do was to actually meet the woman.

"Silly me," Emma said in a flat voice. "Did I forget to mention that trivial thing?"

"Maybe it won't be as bad as you think," Carrie said. "Maybe she's . . . nice."

"And maybe she's loathsome," Emma responded. "My father put her on the phone with me once. Carrie, she squeaked."

"Bad sign," Carrie said solemnly.

"I sort of wish Sam could come to Palm Beach

with me," Emma admitted. "I don't really want to face Valerie alone—but she can't get away from Disney World any earlier."

"Just as well," said Carrie. "Sam is not known for her tact, so she might just stick her foot in her mouth and make the whole thing worse. On the other hand, maybe Valerie will turn out to be a decent person."

"There you go," Emma quipped, "being nice and giving people the benefit of the doubt. You've got to stop that."

Carrie laughed. "But maybe she really is normal!"

"Right," Emma scoffed. "She's only a few years older than we are. Can you see yourself marrying an insecure guy old enough to be your father?"

"Not really," Carrie admitted.

"I rest my case," Emma said. "Valerie is definitely in it for the bucks, and it makes me sick."

Carrie sensed the conversation drifting into rough waters. Fortunately she was adept at steering a smoother course. "So, anyway, where do I fit into this travelogue of yours?"

"Of course we can pick you up in New Haven, but I wish you'd think about meeting us in Orlando. Sam thinks we should check out Daytona on the way up."

"I wish," said Carrie wistfully. "But I don't see how I'm going to meet all my deadlines as it is. You'll just have to give me the gory details once you get here. Which, by the way, will be when?"

Since Emma started spring break one week

ahead of Carrie, they agreed to meet in New Haven the following Friday. They decided on an early lunch at the Hummingbird, one of Carrie's favorite near-campus cafés. That would give Carrie the morning to tidy up loose ends, and the trio could still make Boston for an overnight stay at Emma's apartment. The following day would put them easily into Portland with time to catch the ferry to Sunset Island.

"We'll arrive in time to see the sunset on the island." Carrie sighed longingly. "It's hard to believe this is really going to happen!" She glanced over at her clock. Eight-thirty! She still had to shower, dress, and make a stop at the *Yale Daily News* office before her first class. "I've got to fly, Em!"

"I can't wait to see you!" Emma told Carrie.

"Me, too," Carrie added. She hung up the phone.

Carrie jumped off the bed, her usual efficient self, but suddenly a feeling of loneliness and sadness hit her in such a wave that she had to sit back down again. *Get a grip, Carrie*, she counseled herself, commanding her legs to carry her to the showers.

As the steaming water ran over her body, Carrie thought about how much she missed her two best friends. But she also thought about how much they didn't know about her life. They simply had no concept of the intensity of the life she was leading now. It was a far cry from the seemingly carefree existence they'd enjoyed as au pairs the summer before.

To all outward appearances, Carrie's freshman year at Yale was a complete success. Privately, she felt like a juggler, wondering how much longer she could keep this many plates in the air at once. Her long-distance romance with Billy seemed to intensify with each separation, just as seeing Josh almost every day on campus was creating new and stronger bonds. And jealousy was creeping in from all sides of the triangle.

While Carrie's dream of becoming a photojournalist was moving along on schedule, the burden of success was beginning to weigh on her. Winning a statewide high school photography contest at the end of her senior year had started opening doors, and her summer on Sunset Island had taken her to new heights in her chosen field. Her backstage pictures of the local band Flirting with Danger had been picked up by *Hard Rock News*. And the Templetons, who had hired her as an au pair, had turned out to be the family of legendary rock idol Graham Perry. Respect for Carrie's talents had led Graham to request her as his photographer for an interview in *Rock On*.

Now her coveted position as freshman photographer for the renowned *Yale Daily News* was making her name known around New Haven as a talent on the rise. Clifton Hughes, the newspaper editor, had even sent her to New York on two occasions to cover theater productions involving recent Yale alumni. The trips had been grueling and had required a couple of all-nighters in the study room to keep up with her coursework, but

Hughes had been highly laudatory of the resulting photos.

Carrie turned her face into the spray of the shower and let the water pulse over her head. In spite of studying at least as hard as anyone in her dorm, she was not altogether pleased with her academic performance. Though her first-term grades had been excellent, they had fallen short of the straight-A average she'd been able to maintain in high school.

"My heart jus' bleeds for ya, girl," her friend Mona had quipped on the day grades were posted. "What'd you expect, a cakewalk? This here's Yale, babe."

Mona lived in the room across the hall from Carrie's. She was a National Merit Scholar from Atlanta, a freshman representative on the Minority Council, and handled a part-time job in an off-campus clothing boutique as well. Mona was, in her own words, "bi-dialectal," and could whip into a metropolitan black dialect at the drop of a hat.

"Here you are, a published photographer," Mona had said, "with not one, but two studly dudes fallin' at your feet. You're smart, you come from a good family, you have rich, excitin' friends to go to exclusive islands with—your life is the pits, girl!"

"In other words, I should get over it," Carrie had said ruefully.

"You don't learn to chill out, you gonna grow up

to be a stereotypical uptight white woman," Mona had told her with a twinkle in her eye.

In some part of her mind Carrie knew that even though Mona was teasing her, she was serious, too. *It's just that everything seems so . . . overwhelming sometimes!* she thought.

She shut off the shower and returned to her room.

"Oh my God, I'm a moose," she murmured as she caught sight of herself in the mirror on the wall. She pulled her well-worn terry-cloth bathrobe tight around her, but then took it off and climbed back into bed for a few minutes to contemplate the situation. She could hear Mona's voice in her head, telling her she was nowhere close to being fat. *Unfortunately, I know the truth,* Carrie silently answered the voice. She had gained over fifteen pounds since she'd started college. She pulled the covers up over her head.

It was all so terrible, so scary, so out of control! The form-fitting wardrobe she had finally gotten up the nerve to wear had moved to the rear of her closet, and she was back to wearing loose, baggy clothing.

The cause for the weight gain was no mystery to her: her days were so hectic that she often missed scheduled meals in the dining hall. Instead, she found herself buying junk food, meals and snacks that could be eaten quickly over textbooks or outside the darkroom. Whether she needed to calm down or power up her energies, eating seemed to work.

She was aware that food was becoming a crutch. Just last night, she'd managed to eat an entire medium pizza by herself in the confines of the study room. In spite of how much work she accomplished, she'd gone to bed feeling totally out of control. For Carrie, who was used to being totally in control, the feeling was terrifying.

To make matters worse, she had financial anxieties. The answering machine for the phone in her room had been a necessary extravagance for her newspaper work, but she couldn't really justify the expense of meals outside her meal contract. She felt trapped in a vicious cycle: stress led to eating wrong and eating more, which led to spending money; worry about money only led to more stress. *It's not Sunset Island!* Carrie thought ruefully to herself.

Carrie's family, although fairly well off, was struggling to meet the costs of Yale tuition and living expenses. Carrie's parents had agreed to pay for her first two years at Yale, in hopes that Carrie could qualify for partial help from scholarships or student loans to finish her degree. In addition, she was expected to meet half her monthly expenses, which should have been nominal, considering room and board were included in the deal with her parents.

Any combination of high grades, continued work with the school paper, and outside freelance photography could keep her at Yale without depleting the family college fund, which Carrie's four siblings would eventually need as well. But at this point there were so many factors and so many unknowns that Carrie sometimes felt she was in the first mile of a marathon, and already feeling winded.

A light knock on the door pulled her from the tangle of her thoughts.

"Hope nobody's poutin' in there, 'cause Santa Claus is right outside the door," came the melodious voice of Mona.

Pulling on her robe, Carrie opened the door to see Mona holding a clothes hanger swathed in the trademark print dust cover of Fables, the boutique where she worked.

"And don't you go gettin' all soggy on me—I still owe you for the pics you took of my family while they were here. I've been watchin' this since the day you tried it on, and when they slashed the price, I pounced."

Carrie knew immediately what was inside the garment bag, and was flushed with gratitude at Mona's thoughtfulness. Slipping the garment from its wrapping, she held up the raspberry-colored silk jacket that was cut full in the shoulders, narrowing at the hips. Carrie had been eyeing it since the early spring fashions had arrived at Fables.

Thigh-length, with scalloped side vents, the jacket was beautiful and feminine and would add tremendous versatility to Carrie's wardrobe. She could wear it with jeans, or she could wear it over a skirt for something dressier. Now she found herself wondering if the cut was full enough to hide what Mona called her "curves" and what she thought of as her "bulges."

Holding up the jacket for inspection in the mirror, Carrie had to admit the color flattered her chestnut hair and brown eyes.

"It'll look great with just about everything you own," Mona said. "Unless, of course, you were planning to spend the semester in that bathrobe."

"Yeow!" exclaimed Carrie, remembering the time.

"See you 'round the camp-i," laughed Mona, making for the door.

Carrie stopped her with a gentle touch on the arm. "Thanks, Mona. I really mean it, you're a doll."

"Yeah, yeah, and a real Georgia peach, too," sang Mona, but she grinned broadly and blew Carrie a little kiss before disappearing into her room.

Hurriedly Carrie hung the new jacket in her closet and pulled on her oversized gray cabled sweater with her black stirrup pants and black boots. *Drab*, she thought, trying to picture herself looking bright and slender in the raspberry-colored jacket. *I wish I could peel off about ten pounds before this vacation.*

In less than two weeks, she'd be seeing Billy. In fact, Emma and Sam would be here a week from Friday! They always teased her about her weight worries. Emma, pert and petite, actually *liked* small portions of healthy foods and had never had a weight problem in her life. And Sam, who ate like a horse without seeming to gain an ounce, could probably carry an extra fifteen pounds without it showing on her long frame. It occurred to her, too, that neither of her friends could relate to her financial concerns. In Sam's eyes she was well off, and Emma simply couldn't fathom money problems.

Maybe if I don't eat anything at all for the next week, I can save some money and lose weight, too, she thought as she left her room. Even as she had the thought she knew the plan was ridiculous. For one thing, she knew herself. As soon as she got really hungry all self-control would fly out the window.

"Hi, Carrie," a girl called from across the hall.

Carrie smiled at Sarah Lovett as she walked by her. Sarah was in her biology lab, and she was enviably thin. Even Josh had admitted that he found Sarah very attractive. *Sure,* Carrie thought, *she weighs maybe ninety pounds.*

And then Carrie remembered something that had happened only a few days earlier.

Carrie had been in the girls' bathroom, brushing her teeth before a study date with Josh, when she'd heard someone being sick in one of the stalls. Sarah had emerged from the stall and rinsed out her mouth in a sink a few feet away from Carrie. Their eyes had met in the mirror over the sinks.

"Are you okay?" Carrie had inquired.

"Oh sure, I just ate too much dinner," Sarah had replied.

"And it made you sick?" Carrie had asked wonderingly.

"Of course not, silly! I made myself sick. You think I want all that fried food turning to cellulite while I sleep?"

"But that's terrible for you, isn't it?" Carrie had asked before she could censor herself. "I mean, that's what I've heard," she'd added.

"Only if you do it all the time," Sarah had assured her, reaching into her purse for a lipstick. "I'm too smart to do anything stupid."

"So you just do it sometimes?" Carrie had asked wonderingly.

"Just enough," Sarah had said with a smile of satisfaction. She'd straightened the narrow belt that encircled her size four jeans. "See ya!" she had called, and sauntered out of the bathroom.

Now, watching skinny Sarah Lovett walk confidently down the hall, Carrie thought about what Sarah had told her. Sarah certainly didn't look sick, and she certainly didn't look out of control.

Maybe it isn't such a horrible thing to do, as long as you don't do it very often. Carrie felt a surge of confidence.

Maybe there was a way out after all.

"I must be crazy," sighed Sam as the warm Florida sun bathed her bikini-clad body. "Going north for vacation at this time of year."

"That you're crazy has been well established," answered Danny from his nearby spot on the sand. "In fact, traveling north in April might be a sign that the Sunshine State hasn't warped your brain. There's a world outside of sun, surf, and sand, you know."

"Name one thing Florida doesn't have," challenged Sam.

"Ski season, which I hope I'm not too late to enjoy by the time I get to Vermont. Ever tried skiing?"

"It's not a major pastime back in flat ole Kansas."

"Listen, don't knock it," said Danny, propping himself on one elbow and dribbling a handful of sand on Sam's exposed midriff. "For one thing, you'd make a great-looking ski bunny."

He's flirting with me, thought Sam, and quickly groped for something funny to say. "Somehow I've never pictured myself looking all that hot in traction."

She turned over onto her stomach so she wouldn't have to look at him looking at her. It was weird. Not that she wasn't attracted to Danny, because she was. In fact, in the beginning she'd been crazy for him to make a move on her, but he'd been way too shy.

He was, after all, seriously cute. His auburn-streaked brown hair and sea-green eyes made for a stunning combination. When he smiled, which in Sam's company was often, he had that Tom Cruise magnetism that made his good looks seem boyish and unintimidating. Add to this his natural shyness, and Danny presented a challenge

43

that few girls could resist. Actually, Sam was flattered that he'd chosen to become her friend.

And right now, as Charlie Brown would say, I need all the friends I can get, thought Sam. Now that Danny was finally hinting that he might be interested in more than just friendship, Sam was too afraid to risk what she already had. *I mean, it's a well-documented fact that once a guy is your boyfriend, he can't possibly be your friend anymore*, Sam reasoned.

So far so good, though. Danny didn't show any signs of major disappointment at her sidestepping of his tentative advances. *Well*, thought Sam, *maybe that's because all he really wants to be is my friend, anyway*. The whole thing seemed too complicated.

That day the two of them had made an excursion to Cocoa Beach, a spit of shore just off the east coast of the Florida peninsula, and an easy day trip from Orlando. Danny had the day off from playing Goofy at Disney World, and Sam's waitress shift didn't begin until six o'clock that evening. They'd packed bathing suits and a picnic lunch, had taken the season's first dip in the ocean, and were now enjoying a siesta in the sun before the drive back to Orlando.

"So what's your plan?" Danny queried as he settled back down on the blanket.

"I figure we can stay another half-hour and still make it back on time," Sam said brightly.

"You know that's not what I meant. I meant, what is your plan about your waitress job? You know Big Al isn't going to let you off for two weeks to go on vacation when you just started working there."

"So I'll quit," Sam announced blithely. "Restaurant jobs are a dime a dozen in Orlando."

"Maybe," Danny said, sounding skeptical.

"Listen, Carrie and Emma and I have been planning this trip ever since our Christmas reunion was almost spoiled," Sam said, raising herself up on one elbow. "I'm not giving it up to stay here in a job where I wear ugly shoes and smell like a deep-fat fryer."

"So how are you going to afford this trip?" Danny challenged. "Or, for that matter, your rent when you come back? You *are* coming back, aren't you?"

Sam noted a twinge of apprehension in his voice, and reached out to pat his arm reassuringly. "Yes, Goofy, I'm coming back," she said softly. "As I already told you, Emma's picking me up, so I can stop combing the classifieds for airline tickets. That saving alone should leave a little stash for my return."

"I wish you'd change your mind about lying to your friends," said Danny.

"It's my call," Sam said in a tight voice.

"Sure, but it makes me feel crummy," Danny said. "I'd like to see your friend while she's here, and now *I'll* have to lie to her, too."

"It isn't really a lie," Sam rationalized. "It's more like withholding unpleasant information. I'll

45

level with them once we get to the island." She stood and stretched.

"I don't know—" Danny began doubtfully.

"But I do!" Sam interrupted. She pulled him up from the blanket. "Come on, worrywart. Let's take a stroll and talk about something fun, like our acting careers making us rich and famous someday soon."

Danny agreed—what else could you do with Sam? They started up the beach. The ocean breeze had picked up, forecasting cooler temperatures as evening arrived.

Sam walked into the wind with her arms extended and her head high, shaking her mane of red hair as if the moving air could clear her conscience. *Please get me through this week and on the road before I can tell any more lies*, she prayed. She could think of three she'd told in the last five minutes.

There was no extra money to pay the rent after she returned to Orlando. She wasn't at all sure she was even coming back. And she had no intention of letting on to Carrie and Emma how screwed up her life really was.

FOUR

Brent Cresswell reached over the door of the shiny red Sunbird convertible and placed a finger under his daughter's chin. "Sure I can't buy you breakfast before you get on the road?" he asked for the second time that morning.

"Really, Daddy, you've bought me more than enough," Emma answered, tapping the steering wheel for emphasis. "And I really do need to get started. I never dreamed Orlando was such a long drive from Palm Beach. I guess I've done most of my stateside traveling on planes."

Emma was babbling and she knew it. This was an awkward good-bye, and she couldn't fool her father any more than she could fool herself. Still, some sense of propriety drove both of them to try to salvage, here at the eleventh hour, what had been a relentlessly uncomfortable visit.

If he says one word about how upset Valerie will be that she couldn't drag her sorry self out of bed to see me off, I will vomit right here on this sparkling white upholstery, thought Emma.

"Listen, princess," her father began, "I meant what I said about us becoming a real family again."

Again? thought Emma. *We were never a real family.*

"I don't want to lose track of you," he continued.

Emma thought of all the birthdays and holidays when her father had had no idea where she was. *A little late for that, isn't it?* she wanted to tell him. *I'm eighteen years old!*

"Stay in touch, Emma. Maybe we can spend some real time together next time I'm up north."

Though she knew he had ulterior motives, Emma realized her father was making a genuine try at affection, and she felt a lump rise in her throat. He certainly hadn't been the best father in the world, but he was hers.

"Sounds good," she managed. "See you." For a split second she wished she had the kind of family that said, "I love you," but she took her foot off the brake, letting the car glide slowly forward toward the street.

Emma glanced back once in the rearview mirror, and it occurred to her that her father looked a little forlorn standing in the driveway. He gave a subdued wave. She honked the horn as the car accelerated, and he disappeared from view.

Born and raised a lady, Emma drove in silence until she had gotten on Interstate 95 and was certain passing traffic would drown out her voice. Then she let fly with every foul word she'd ever even thought of using. "Valerie Johnson," she concluded, gritting her teeth.

Valerie Johnson was her father's—she could barely form the word, even in her mind—*fiancée*. She was even more awful than Emma's worst imaginings. Emma had given herself a pep talk on the plane to Florida and convinced herself that she owed it to her father to give Valerie the benefit of the doubt.

But after five minutes in Valerie's company, Emma had known she would have to throw in the towel.

Standing beside her father in the gate area had been a slightly chubby young woman dressed in a style that fell somewhere between Shirley Temple and Minnie Mouse. While everyone in sight had been in typical Florida casual attire, Valerie had dressed for the occasion in a black flared miniskirt with a white lace hem, a black-and-white polka-dot puffy-sleeved top, and a yellow bolero jacket. Black granny heels, ruffled white party socks, and a polka-dot hairband with an oversized bow completed the ensemble. Her hair fell in bright yellow curls to her shoulders, framing a round face with too much makeup and a constant expression of surprise.

Emma had felt her stomach drop.

"And this, of course, is Valerie," her father had announced with pride after a warm embrace for Emma.

"You don't look anything like I thought you

would!" Valerie had squeaked, her penciled eyebrows shooting up in amazement.

And you look just how you sound—it's amazing! Emma had thought to herself. What she had actually said aloud was something more along the lines of "nice to meet you."

While her father was loading Emma's bag into the trunk, Valerie had turned and leaned over the back of the Lincoln's front seat, her overly mascaraed eyes peering at Emma's hairline. "Your color's fabulous! Who does it?"

"Nature," Emma had answered truthfully.

Valerie had clapped her little hands together with glee. "Good for you! I've used that line myself for years," she'd added confidentially.

Brent had beamed at them both as he got in and started the car. "Well, I'm glad to see my two girls are getting along so well."

"Oh, we are, Brentsie!" Valerie had assured him breathlessly.

Brentsie?

"I thought we'd go straight to the showroom and get you started on picking out a car, Emma," her father had said over his shoulder. "If we get lucky, you'll be driving your new set of wheels by lunchtime. I have an afternoon appointment and thought you girls might like to get in some shopping."

"Glorious!" Valerie had chirped. "Emma can help me pick out a few more things for my trousseau!"

Trousseau? As in wedding? As in Brentsie and Valerie?

Of course, she'd known about it, but deep in her heart Emma had hoped it wasn't really true. But sitting in the back seat, she hadn't been able to ignore the large diamond that the yellow-curled woman flashed on her left hand.

Car shopping had been quick. Trousseau shopping had taken forever. It seemed that Brentsie had put no limits on Valerie's charge card. It had been obvious to Emma that Valerie was a woman who lived for conspicuous consumption.

Now—was it only twenty-four hours later?— Emma was just thankful to be putting the whole hideous experience behind her. That her father was going to marry that moron was just too excruciating to believe.

Emma wheeled into the parking lot of a roadside diner where a giant orange the size of a hot-air balloon promised fresh-squeezed orange juice and home-style breakfasts.

Two young guys in an old station wagon with a couple of surfboards on the top were just pulling out, and as Emma got out of the car they honked appreciatively at her—or was it just the sporty red convertible? The guy in the passenger seat leaned out the window toward her. Emma smiled to herself as he pretended to wrench his heart from his chest and toss it to her.

He's cute too, she admitted. Then and there Emma resolved to forget about her neurotic parents and their horrid choice in mates. That was *their* problem. She was young, free, rich, and on vacation. It was time to leave yesterday's baggage behind and let the good times roll.

Sitting in one of the old-fashioned booths with a tableside jukebox, Emma thought of Sam, only a few hours away and awaiting her arrival. By that night they'd be at Stingray's dancing with all those cute guys.

For the first time in twenty-four hours, she had a real appetite.

"And that's exactly why we can't go to Stingray's," Sam finished telling Danny. "How could I have been so stupid?"

"Oh, what a tangled web we weave, eh?" quipped Danny. "You may want to blow off your friends from Disney World, but how do you know Emma's not counting on going out tonight? You're the one who planned it."

"That was before I reorganized my brain cells," retorted Sam. "Obviously I can't take the chance that someone will tell her I'm not with the troupe anymore. Besides, I told her we should head on up to Daytona and cruise the scene there. I'll just convince her we should go right there and not spend any time here in Orlando."

"Let me get this straight," Danny began. "You're willing to deprive me of Emma's company, and a last night with you; you're willing to give up partying with a lot of people who like you a lot and are always asking how you're doing—and all to keep up appearances for someone who is, supposedly, one of your very best friends?" He shook his head. "Maybe you'd better rethink your priorities."

"Maybe you'd better loosen your cassock, pal," scoffed Sam. "If I need a priest, I'll go to confession."

Danny's expression told her that her words had stung, and Sam felt a stab of regret. *How can I hurt Danny like this?* she thought. But another voice in her head countered, *I have simply got to get out of this town!*

Danny had picked her up an hour ago, and they were now relaxing on the balcony of his second-floor apartment after stashing a few of Sam's things in the storage area below. Sam's excuse was that her roommates always borrowed her clothes, and she didn't want to leave her stuff lying around to be picked over while she was out of town.

The truth was that although she didn't have many possessions, she might want to reclaim them someday, and didn't want to have to face her roommates if she skated on their lease. Danny was acting a little strange, but he hadn't asked her too many questions, at least until he'd found out she was more or less breaking their date for that night.

"Look, I'm sorry I barked at you, Danny. You're the best friend I have in this town, but I just need to get out for a while. Try to understand."

"I just worry about you, that's all." Danny

sighed. "By the way, how did it go with Big Al?"

"Amazingly well!" Sam said brightly. "He said he'd have liked a little more notice, but was going to have to let someone go anyway—it's late in the season and he probably shouldn't have hired me to begin with. He told me to check with him when I come back because"—here Sam imitated the New-Yorker-moved-south—"he liked my style and in this crazy business, you never know."

She didn't mention that she'd told Big Al she was going north to audition for a Broadway musical. She wasn't sure he'd have been so understanding about a vacation with her friends.

Sam's mental review of what she hoped was her last lie in Orlando was interrupted by the blare of a car horn. Both she and Danny were on their feet in time to see the red convertible round the corner into the parking lot of Danny's building, where Sam had instructed Emma to meet her. Emma was waving from behind the wheel.

"Too cool!" cheered Sam as Emma pulled up to the curb below. She jumped up, raced through Danny's apartment, and went down the stairs two at a time.

Emma leapt out of the car and threw her arms around Sam. Emma surprised even herself with that gesture. Normally very reserved, she just couldn't believe how happy she was to see Sam again.

"You look fabulous!" Emma cried, holding Sam at arm's length. Sam had on white cotton shorts and a rayon shirt featuring a puffy pink poodle being lassoed by some cowboys. The back of the shirt read, CITIZENS FOR A POODLE-FREE MONTANA.

"It's the tan," Sam said with a grin. "As for you, you look the same, meaning perfect." Emma had on fitted pink cotton pants with a matching pink-and-white cotton shirt. It looked deceptively simple, but Sam knew it probably came from some designer resort collection and cost a mint.

"Goofy!" Emma said cheerfully, smiling at Danny. "Oh, wait, I remember," she added playfully. "I'm only supposed to call you Goofy when you're wearing your Goofy costume."

Danny smiled shyly. "Hey, I'm over that," he told her. "It's great to see you, Emma."

"So enough of the greetings," Sam said. "I want a ride in this puppy!" She jumped over the door and landed smoothly in the back seat. "Coming?" she called.

"As long as I'm driving toward a restaurant," Emma said. "I haven't eaten since breakfast." Emma and Danny got into the car.

"Hey, this could be a first," Sam called into the wind as they drove out of the parking lot. "Emma Cresswell admits that she's hungry. We'll go to Tattoo," Sam decreed. "*Très* hip. Turn right at the corner."

"I can't wait to see all your friends at Stingray's tonight," Emma exclaimed as they cruised along. "I had so much fun there the last time."

No one said anything. Emma thought she saw Danny's cheeks flush. *Isn't he coming with us to*

Stingray's? she wondered. *Maybe I just stuck my foot in my mouth.*

"Yum, I'm starved," Sam said a few minutes later as they scanned the menus at Tattoo. "The Tattoo burger is to die for," she suggested.

"Oh, I'll just have a salad," Emma said absentmindedly. "Hey, how about if we order some wine? It's on me!"

"None for me," Danny said. "It gives me a headache when I've been in the sun."

"I'll pass, too," Sam said.

"Oh, come on," Emma chided. "We're celebrating!"

The three of them ordered their food and Emma insisted upon a bottle of Sauvignon blanc. The waitress poured some in all three of their glasses, and Emma lifted hers for a toast.

"To great friends and great adventures," she pronounced.

They all clinked glasses and sipped the wine.

Sam pushed her glass away and reached for her burger. "Not that I don't appreciate the symbolism," she said, "but I don't travel well on alcohol."

"Who's traveling?" said Emma, sipping her wine. "We don't have to go any farther than Stingray's and your apartment."

A look passed between Sam and Danny.

"Well, see, the thing is, I was thinking how cool it would be to just, like, you know, leave for Daytona," Sam began.

"But I thought we were going out with your friends tonight," Emma said, puzzled.

"Yeah, but it's . . . my apartment!" Sam said, thinking fast. "My roommates are in town tonight and they're being really bitchy about my having anyone stay over."

"So we'll stay at a hotel," Emma suggested.

"I'm on a budget Emma, even if you're not," Sam said stiffly.

Emma bit her lip. Sam was right. She probably felt bad about her apartment situation, and Emma was just embarrassing her.

"Hey, listen, Sam, it's fine if we leave tonight," Emma said softly. "Honest."

Sam got very busy with her french fries. At that particular moment she wasn't very proud of herself. She'd told yet another lie and had made Emma feel terrible, just to manipulate things so they were the way she wanted them to be.

"So listen," Emma began brightly, eager to change the mood, "my father gave me a brand-new credit card for this trip. We should make good use of it!"

"Speaking of your father," Sam said, "how was the trip?"

Emma refilled her wineglass and rolled her eyes. "Let's just say that the story would ruin all our appetites. So I'll save it." The wine was making her feel warm and fuzzy, and she didn't want to lose the effect. Quickly she changed topics and filled Sam in on the itinerary she'd planned.

"I didn't realize you were stopping in Boston," said Danny. "I'm flying up there to meet my friend Kevin. We're going from there up to Vermont for some skiing."

That's a long speech for Danny, Emma thought. "Maybe we can meet up," she suggested. "It'd be fun. Carrie will be with us by then."

"Party at Emma's mansion!" announced Sam. "It is a mansion, isn't it?" she asked Emma. "I'll be so bummed if it isn't a mansion."

"It's a mansion," Emma assured her. She swallowed the last of the wine—*no point in wasting it*, she thought—and grabbed the check. She gave Danny her phone number in Boston while waiting for the waitress to return with her credit card.

"So listen, I'm going to a friend's around the corner," Danny told Emma when they got to the parking lot. "It was great to see you."

"You, too," Emma said warmly.

"And have a great trip," he added.

"It will be awesome, amazing, and life-altering," Sam assured him.

"You take care," Danny told Sam in a low voice, brushing her cheek with a kiss. "I'm going to miss you."

Sam looked wistful as she watched Danny jog away.

"You really like him, huh?" Emma asked her.

"He's a great guy," Sam said, "but he's just a friend."

"You sure?" Emma asked.

"Sure I'm sure," Sam said. "Listen, I'm dying to get my hands on the wheel of your car. What say I drive us back to my digs so we can pick up my stuff, and then we hit the road?"

"You're on," Emma agreed. If Sam hadn't said she'd drive, Emma would have asked her to, since Sam had barely sipped her wine and Emma had had more than two full glasses.

"You would not believe what I went through in Palm Beach," Emma yelled over the rock music Sam had tuned in on the radio. Emma described the whole horrible ordeal to her.

"Brentsie?" Sam guffawed. "Was she serious?"

"It gets worse!" Emma said. "After we went shopping we were sitting around the pool, and she made some comment about how 'sexually deprived' my father had been until he met her."

"Gross!" Sam screeched. "Why didn't you do the world a favor and push her into the pool with a rock tied around her neck?"

Emma laughed. "I just can't believe my father is going to marry her!" she marveled.

"It *is* amazingly hideous," Sam agreed. She thought back to her meeting with Emma's mother the previous summer, as well as an almost disastrous encounter with Kat Cresswell's fiancé, Austin Payne. Interestingly enough, thought Sam, Austin was around the same age as Valerie. And in his own way, just as excruciating. Sam knew Emma must be totally mortified. *At least my parents are normal*, Sam thought. *Boring, but normal*.

"You got along okay with your dad, though?" Sam asked.

"Sure," Emma said bitterly. "But he pulled a Katerina on me."

"A *what?*" Sam yelled over the radio.

"In other words, he had an ulterior motive, which is more often my mother's territory," Emma explained. She turned down the radio. "He took me out for lunch—Valerie had an appointment for a manicure—and he actually asked me to testify against my mother in the divorce hearing!"

"That sucks, Em," Sam commiserated. She pulled up in front of her apartment building.

Emma was staring at her hands, willing herself not to cry. "I just couldn't believe it!" she said, shaking her head sadly.

"So what are you supposed to be testifying to?" Sam asked.

"That she hasn't been a loving parent, if that isn't the pot calling the kettle black!" Emma said bitterly. "He's so afraid she'll keep the entire family fortune for herself, he's grasping at straws to show she might be mentally incompetent."

"God, Em, I don't know what to say," Sam began.

"Then he had the nerve to tell me how much he wants me back in his life," Emma continued. "What a joke! I had to have two glasses of wine over lunch just to keep from killing him."

"I don't know what to say, except that parents suck," Sam said mildly. "It's some kind of a disease. It's not just your parents."

"Oh, come on, Sam," Emma said, finally lifting

her eyes to look at Sam. "Your parents would never do anything like this, would they?"

"No, I guess not," Sam admitted. "But believe me when I tell you they have done more than their fair share of embarrassing things to me in my life."

"I . . . I really wanted to tell him something about my life, you know?" Emma continued earnestly. "I wanted him to know about the volunteer work I'm going to start doing with kids in inner-city Washington. I thought he might be happy about it. But we never got a chance to talk without Valerie around, and all she wanted to talk about was shopping."

"Look Em, let me run in and get my stuff and we'll get going, okay?" Sam asked. "We can talk more on the way."

Emma nodded her assent. She looked so forlorn that Sam reached over and touched Emma's hand for a moment. "Listen, it'll be okay. We're going on an incredible adventure, right?"

Emma smiled gratefully. "Right," she agreed. "I'm acting like a little idiot. It's probably just the wine I drank."

A few minutes later they had pulled away from the curb and were headed for Daytona. Sam did most of the talking. It amazed even her how easy it was to lie about her life and pretend that she was still dancing at Disney World. She rationalized that it was because she had a superior imagination and was going to turn out to be a majorly successful actress in the long run.

By the time they reached Daytona, Emma had fallen asleep, and Sam had to negotiate the thronging streets and the plethora of No Vacancy signs alone. She hadn't considered that spring break in Daytona Beach was practically synonymous with No Vacancy signs.

Exasperated, she was finally forced to settle for a dingy motel more than a few blocks inland, with the dubious name of the Reefer. Emma woke long enough to hand Sam her credit card and instruct her to tell the desk clerk she'd sign the slip in the morning.

Emma made straight for bed, saying she was exhausted and had a raging headache. Sam set out to do some exploring, but was quickly intimidated by the jeering groups of drunk guys who seemed to be hanging from the street signs on every corner. She bought a takeout sandwich and a Coke, and ended up watching an old movie on TV, with Emma mumbling in her sleep in the next bed.

Sam pictured Danny back in Orlando, probably watching the same movie. Danny loved old movies.

Some incredible vacation, she thought morosely. *Here I am in a seedy little hotel that smells of roach spray, sitting next to a passed-out friend and thinking about Goofy!*

FIVE

"Sam?"

Sam heard the voice through a dream in which she was back at Big Al's, waiting on Mr. Christopher. She had turned from the table after apologizing for bringing the wrong order. Then he said, "Can't you do anything right?" The voice was different, and looking back, she saw not Mr. Christopher but Danny, his expression full of reproach. Now someone at the next table was calling her name again, and Sam spun around to see that the party of twelve was her dance troupe from Disney World.

"I'm sorry!" she cried out to their questioning faces. Her words seemed to be struggling up through layers of Jell-O.

"Don't be sorry, just get up!"

The laughing voice was Emma's, and a second later Sam's dream receded into white light as Emma opened the drapes, flooding the motel room with sunshine.

Sam pulled herself to a sitting position, and

rubbed her face. "Aargh! Thanks for waking me. I was having the worst dream."

"About what?" Emma was bustling around the room in a shell-pink mini shirtdress, drinking coffee and looking like she'd been awake for hours.

"The details aren't too clear," lied Sam, "but I was feeling sort of lost and ashamed at the same time." She stood and stretched luxuriously. "What time is it, anyway?"

"Quarter past seven."

"In the morning? I didn't know there was a seven-fifteen in the morning!" With both the dance revue and the restaurant shifts, Sam had become accustomed to working at night and sleeping late in the morning.

"You were the one who wanted to check out spring break in Daytona Beach, remember?"

"As I seem to recall, you were the one who slept through our only Saturday night here," rejoined Sam.

Ducking her head guiltily, Emma said, "I'm really sorry about that, Sam. I guess I was just stressed out from dealing with my family. They exhaust me sometimes."

Sam interjected, "Funny, but I would have blamed the wine, myself."

"Oh, that," breezed Emma. "Well, I'm definitely not drinking any alcohol today." She dismissed the subject with a wave of her hand and continued, "I've already signed for the room, and they recommended a good place for breakfast.

Why don't you take a shower? I'll be reading my book out by the pool."

Sam did, and felt much more alive by the time they were strolling the few blocks to the waterfront. The refuse of the previous night's revelry still littered the streets, but the town looked harmless enough in the morning light. With the last remnants of her nightmare fading thankfully into oblivion, Sam found a renewed enthusiasm for life in general and their road trip in particular. She was carrying the road atlas, which she'd asked Emma to get from the car. She'd been so anxious to get out of Orlando that she hadn't really paid attention when Emma had described their route.

She glanced through it as they ate breakfast. Mopping up the last of her huevos rancheros with a crust of toast, Sam asked the waitress for a refill on her coffee. Emma had ordered whole-grain muffins with fresh fruit and yogurt, and was still mincing through her meal.

"Don't you ever just want to wolf down a really greasy burger and a double order of cheese fries?" Sam asked her.

Emma gave Sam a horrified look. "Why would I want to do a thing like that?"

Sam shook her head and buried her head back in the atlas. "I swear, you are missing the gene for junk food," she mumbled. "Okay, the way I see it, we hang on the beach this morning, break a few hearts, and then head for Savannah after lunch, right?" Sam asked.

"Right," answered Emma. "We stay on Interstate 95 all the way to New Haven, and since we left ahead of schedule we have plenty of time to spend an entire day somewhere along the way. Just so we're in New York by Thursday night. We have to meet Carrie in New Haven by lunchtime Friday."

"Ooh! Let's spend a day in the mountains!"

"There aren't any mountains along I–95."

"C'mon, Em," wheedled Sam, "I've never seen mountains except from the air. The highest point in Kansas is a corn tassel."

Emma thought of the Alps, which she'd had the privilege of enjoying a number of times since her childhood. It was hard for her to imagine anyone her age who had never been to the mountains.

"Let's think about it when we get to Savannah," she suggested. "I don't want us driving more than six hours a day, and I'm not sure we can stick to that if we change our route."

"Hey, it's your wheels and your credit card!" Sam said with a shrug.

Emma paid the check and left a tip, then turned to see Sam slip an extra dollar onto the table.

Looking a little chagrined, Sam explained, "I always tip twenty percent for good service. Nobody can live very well on fifteen, and it's a rough job, anyway."

"How would you know?" laughed Emma.

"I guess if I'd been born with a silver spoon in my mouth, I wouldn't," Sam snapped.

"What was that for?" Emma asked, hurt.

Sam sighed. "Ignore me," she said, linking her arm in Emma's. "I'm a product of unbalanced hormones."

Once they were out of the restaurant and on their way back to the motel, Sam took on a boisterous good cheer. By now there were more people to be seen on the streets, and almost everyone nodded or smiled as they walked by. Sam sprouted a running commentary on all sightings of the opposite sex as they went.

"Oh baby oh baby oh baby!" Sam murmured as a dark-haired guy who looked like a model for tanning products walked by.

"Help you wax your board, dude?" she mouthed as they passed a long-haired blond surfer.

Sam made a pouty face and said, "Poor baby, let me put some sunscreen on those shoulders," when she spotted a fair-skinned, redheaded guy who looked like he'd stayed on the beach too long the day before.

At one point, the girls passed one of the previous night's casualties, a bleary-eyed guy who left an aroma of stale beer in his wake and looked like he'd slept in a gutter.

"Sorry, but I don't date outside my species," Sam stage-whispered in Emma's direction.

Sam and Emma were still laughing as they reached the motel and changed into their bathing suits. They threw on coverups and hurriedly packed their belongings into the car. There had still been parking places at the public beach when they finished breakfast, but those would go quickly now that the sun was getting high.

They had just found a spot, parked, and were loading books, towels, and lotion into Emma's canvas beachbag when a car horn honked and a deep voice called, "Hey, look who's here!"

Emma glanced up and was surprised to see the guys with the surfboards from the breakfast stop the day before. Suddenly remembering the show of appreciation she'd received from the dark-haired guy, Emma blushed furiously and pretended to be looking for something still in the car.

"Those guys are waving at us," said Sam. "Do you know them?"

"Not really. They honked at me when I stopped for breakfast yesterday. They must have been on their way up here, too."

"So wave back, for cryin' out loud! They're adorable and they have surfboards!"

"Oh, I don't know . . ." Emma started.

Sam reached over and took Emma's elbow, propelling it upward until the hand at the end appeared to wave awkwardly. Sam performed a more controlled version with her free hand, calling, "Hi, guys. Need some help with those boards?"

"We can manage the boards, but if you'll find us a spot on the beach, we'll share our cooler with you," returned the driver, a freckle-faced blonde whom Sam thought resembled Michael J. Fox. But taller, she noted with satisfaction.

The other guy was not much taller than Emma, and had jet-black hair, almond-shaped brown eyes with long black lashes, and a creamy brown complexion. His compact body rippled with muscles as he helped unfasten the cords that secured the surfboards.

"I'm Buddy," he said as Sam and Emma passed by the station wagon, "and that's Jack."

"Hi, Jack," said Sam over the roof of the car. She turned to include Buddy in the introduction. "I'm Sam, and this is Emma."

Jack nodded and smiled as Buddy reached out to shake hands. Sam got a firm grip and a hello, but she noted that Buddy's hand lingered for a moment around Emma's, and his voice had a melodic, reverent tone as he said, "Emma."

"He likes you," she whispered, nudging Emma as they walked through the sand.

"Sam, really! He doesn't even know me."

"He doesn't have to know you to like you the way I'm talking about," said Sam.

The girls spread their towels and removed their coverups. Emma had on a hot pink two-piece, shot through with metallic gold; the bottom had a fashionably high waist that hid her navel. Sam's vivid deep purple suit was solid-colored and one piece, but was more revealing than Emma's: it was cut extremely high in the leg, low in the bust, and slashed out on both sides to show most of Sam's long torso.

Emma opened her book, but Sam pulled on her

baseball cap and studied Buddy and Jack as they made for the water with their boards.

"Wanna go for a swim?" she asked Emma.

"We just got here."

"So? The waves won't be this good again until late afternoon. I think we've got a chance for some free surfing lessons."

"You go ahead. I'll just read awhile."

"Suit yourself," said Sam. The next moment she was racing for the water and splashing in with a flourish of her long arms.

Emma spent the next half-hour immersed in her book, *G Is for Gumshoe*. The story involved a female private investigator who drove a beat-up old Volkswagen bug, was confidently independent, and had all kinds of adventures. Though she knew the investigator was a fictitious character, Emma suspected there really were women like her. The thought of spending three more years majoring in French at Goucher College was stifling.

"Yahoo! Hey, Emma!"

Emma looked up just in time to see Sam wobbling atop a surfboard before a wave caught her from behind and tumbled her into the water. The board drifted toward shore as Emma shaded her eyes and searched for a glimpse of Sam. Within seconds she spotted Sam's sleek red head bobbing along the surface, and recognized Jack swimming over to join her.

A shadow crossed Emma's towel. Looking up, she saw it was Buddy. As he shook the salt water from his hair, the beads of water picked up the sun and created a twinkling arc.

"So what do you say, Emma?" he said with a smile. "Ready to try it yourself?"

"I—I don't know how," Emma stammered.

"You can swim, can't you?"

"Well, sure."

"If you can swim, and you can stand up, you can surf." Buddy reassured her. "The waves are too small to be a challenge, but I'd have fun teaching you. That is, if you want me to."

Emma was about to demur when her eye fell on her book, which she'd tossed aside when on the lookout for Sam. *Why not?* she thought. *If I'm ever going to have any real adventures, I'll have to try some things I've never done before.*

"Sure, okay," she told Buddy.

"Attagirl!" he cheered, and placed his hand lightly on the small of her back as he guided her toward the water.

Surfing turned out to be harder than it looked. Emma was cautious not to let the board slip out from under her, but she didn't trust herself to rise above an awkward crouch. Sam, with her dance training, had excellent balance but was a hotdogger—always trying for a faster, more exciting ride. Her physical control let her fall harmlessly when she wiped out, which she did predictably. Emma noticed that Jack was always nearby to encourage her when she surfaced.

Laughing and winded, the foursome took a

break, and the girls were astounded to find it was almost noon.

"No sense in rushing," Sam said. "Savannah will still be there."

They brought sandwiches from a stand down the beach, and the boys went to their car for the cooler.

"Let's stay, Emma!" entreated Sam when the boys were out of earshot. "This could be the night!"

"For what?" Emma asked.

"You know . . ." said Sam.

"Sam! You just met this guy!"

"That's what I mean. It's perfect! No ties, no commitment, no big deal. Aren't you tired of being a virgin?"

"Sometimes. But I've waited this long, I want to at least start out with someone I care about."

"What's not to care about?" said Sam, watching Jack's body as he and Buddy approached. "Anyway, he's really nice."

"We are going to Savannah—*today*," Emma said firmly.

After lunch, Sam and Jack decided to walk down the beach. Emma and Buddy stayed behind and talked. Buddy was from Miami, and his mother was Cuban. *So that's where he gets that exotic allure,* thought Emma. He and Jack were both at the University of Florida in Miami, and had come north to Daytona to enjoy the hedonism of spring break in a collegiate hot spot.

"I wish you'd think of staying over," Buddy

said, grasping Emma's hand and running his thumb softly over her knuckles, "You won't be in Savannah in time to see anything, anyway."

"We have other people depending on us to keep to our schedule, though," said Emma, giving his hand a quick squeeze before releasing it to delve into her bag. She couldn't deny that his touch had sent a shiver of desire through her, but it reminded her of Kurt, awaiting her arrival on Sunset Island.

Emma found her watch and was distressed to see that it was almost two o'clock. Where was Sam?

"If you change your mind, I'd be happy to take you to dinner," Buddy offered. "I thought you were beautiful the first moment I laid eyes on you yesterday." He looked her straight in the eye.

"Oh Buddy, that's so sweet, but . . . look—there they are!"

Emma had spied Sam and Jack strolling unhurriedly near the water. They had their arms around each other, and as Emma watched, they kissed languidly. Right out in public—that Sam!

Feeling like a small yapping dog trying to herd some sheep, Emma finally managed to get Sam and their beach gear up to the car, with Buddy and Jack in tow. Emma allowed Buddy a brief kiss, then swung into the driver's seat, and jangled the keys until Sam broke off her passionate embrace with Jack and hopped in the passenger side.

Emma steeled herself for criticism, but Sam

was uncharacteristically quiet as they wheeled toward the interstate.

"Thanks, Emma," Sam finally said serenely. "Nothing Jack and I could have done would have been as romantic as that walk on the beach before driving off into the sunset."

"You're not mad?" Emma asked.

"Nope. He was actually too nice a guy to love and leave. Guess I'm getting addicted to unfulfilled prophecy."

Emma tuned in a classical station, and before long, Sam was snoozing as Brahms took them north in the waning light.

Carrie braced herself against the wall of the toilet stall and stared wonderingly into the vortex of the emptying bowl. The back of her throat was burning, and her eyes stung with tears. But the sky hadn't opened, thunder hadn't rolled, and lightning hadn't struck her down. She got control of her breathing, wiped her eyes, and hurried from the stall.

I don't ever have to do this again, she thought, but oddly, she felt a sense of accomplishment—she hadn't thought she could do it at all.

She was toweling off her face at the sink when the door opened and Sarah Lovett breezed in. Sarah gave her a knowing smile, and Carrie felt that she and the willowy girl had a shared secret.

She returned to her room feeling like a different person from the one who'd left only a few minutes ago. *I'm definitely not going to make a habit of this*, she assured herself. But she had to admit she took satisfaction in throwing the donut box into the trash, knowing all that grease and sugar were no longer in her body.

Her mind groped for an exact word to express the feeling, and finally settled on *powerful*.

Sam didn't wake up until they stopped for gas. She offered to drive, but Emma said she felt up to it, and Savannah was only another hour away. They spent the time speculating on how Carrie was doing, and tossing around ideas for the big party they'd been planning since Christmas.

In Savannah they stopped for directions to the D'Urbanville, a grand old Southern hotel where Emma knew her mother's friends stayed when they were in town. She figured she and Sam deserved some luxury at least every other night.

The hotel had a gracious circular drive, with a canopy and a uniformed doorman. Azaleas bloomed profusely in every direction, their brilliant magenta accentuated by the hotel's subtle lighting. Emma left the car to be unloaded by the bellman and parked by the valet. With Sam rubbernecking at her heels, she made her way through the richly appointed lobby to negotiate a room with the desk clerk.

"We'd like a suite if you have one available—with a hot tub, if possible."

"Certainly. Will you be paying by credit card?"

"Yes, please," said Emma, turning to Sam. "Sam, you have the card."

"No, I don't." There was a moment of stunned silence before Sam blubbered, "Didn't you pick it up when you signed us out this morning?"

"You left it at the desk last night?" Emma intoned incredulously.

"Well, how should I know? I've never had a credit card."

The clerk was now regarding them somewhat doubtfully.

Emma reached into her purse and said crisply, "I do have another card."

The clerk set to making their arrangements as Emma fumed in silence and Sam stood by dejectedly.

"I'm really, really sorry, Emma. I feel so stupid."

"It wouldn't be so bad if it weren't my father's card," Emma admitted. "The last thing I want is to have to call him about this."

As the clerk handed over their receipt and keys, Emma's eyes scanned the lobby.

"Come on," she said, grabbing Sam by the arm. "We can think this through in the bar. I don't know about you, but I need a glass of wine."

SIX

Sam snuggled her shoulders deeper into the hotel's voluptuous pillows and tried to concentrate on her book. She hadn't been able to get into the acting book Danny had loaned her, something called *The Method*, but had thought this gothic romance would surely whisk her into dreamland, or at least fantasyland. But her thoughts kept returning to Emma. Emma wasn't acting like Emma. Didn't she know it was Sam who was supposed to do crazy things?

The credit card crisis had been resolved when Emma found she had the receipt from the motel, and therefore the card number. She'd used the phone in the bar to dial the toll-free number for reporting lost or stolen cards. They'd both been relieved when there had been no need to get in touch with Brent Cresswell after all.

But the incident had gotten Emma back on the subject of her screwed-up family. She had ordered a glass of wine in the bar, and a second to take with her into the dining room, where she'd barely touched the small Caesar salad she'd ordered for dinner. Sam, who had pigged out as usual, had opted for an after-dinner walk through the hotel gardens, saying she'd meet Emma upstairs for a dip in the hot tub.

The gardens were beautiful, and Sam had lingered there. When she'd returned to the suite, she made straight for the tiled solarium, where she could hear the soft bubbling of the steaming tub. She had found Emma climbing groggily out of the tub.

"So how's the water?" Sam had inquired gaily just as Emma slid to a sitting position on the bench outside the tub, then leaned forward to let her head rest on her knees.

"Oh Sam, I don't feel so good," had come Emma's weak and muffled voice.

Sam had placed a hand on Emma's shoulder, which burned to the touch.

"You're overheated!" she had cried. "Wait right here."

Sam knew from dance rehearsals that heat exhaustion could make you feel faint, dizzy, and nauseated. She also recalled hearing that it wasn't a good idea to sit in a hot tub after drinking alcohol; you might doze off and not realize you were getting dangerously overheated.

Sam had flown to the kitchenette and filled a large glass with water, then raced back to find that Emma had pulled herself to a sitting position. Sam had grabbed a towel from the nearby stack and placed it lightly over Emma's shoulders.

"You need to cool off, but not too fast," Sam had counseled. "And you need water. Here, drink this."

Emma had done as she was told, then let Sam lead her to her bed.

"I'm fine now, Sam, really. Just a little woozy," she had said, propping herself against the quilted headboard. She'd attempted a smile, but wasn't very successful. Her cheeks still burned too brightly. "I was just trying to relax and forget about my family for a while."

Sam had sat down at the foot of Emma's bed. "Look, Emma, I don't want to get on your case about this, but, well, you're letting your parents drive you crazy!"

"Yeah, you're right," Emma had agreed. "I've just got to forget all about them."

"That's the spirit!" Sam had said.

"I can't let them ruin my vacation," Emma had said vehemently.

And mine, Sam had added in her mind.

So, Sam thought as she stretched in the enormous hotel bed, everything would be okay. But something was nagging at Sam. It felt like Emma was saying the right things, but she didn't really mean them. Also, Sam had never seen Emma drink like she'd been doing over the last couple of days. It all seemed really weird.

Sam closed her book and set it aside. The romance novel couldn't help with this dilemma.

But the plantation-style furnishings of the room brought to mind one of her favorite literary quotes of all time, a well-known Scarlett O'Hara line from *Gone With The Wind*. *I can't think about this right now,* she reasoned. *I'll think about this . . . tomorrow.*

With that, she fluffed the pillows, turned out the light, and settled in to rest up for a new day.

"Open up! Police!"

In this dream, Sam was in a queen-size four-poster bed with a canopy. She couldn't figure out where the police came into the story.

An insistent pounding brought her fully to her senses, and she realized this wasn't a dream at all. She was in her room in the suite they'd rented at the D'Urbanville, and as near as she could figure, the police were just outside the door.

The pounding came again. "Open up in there!"

Sam felt a twinge of panic. Surely the police wouldn't be at her door unless she'd done something wrong, but what could it be? It had to be the wrong room, that was all. She was trying to find her voice and remember where she'd tossed her robe, when she heard the loud jangle of keys on the other side of the suite's door.

"We're coming in!" said the same authoritative voice. A moment later the door opened, and footsteps crossed the suite's living room. Suddenly Sam's bedroom door was flung open.

As Sam clutched the bedclothes to her chest a flashlight beam slid across the room and centered on her face. Blinded by the intense light, she managed to sputter, "It's just me!"

"Emma Cresswell?" inquired the voice behind the light.

"Samantha Bridges," squeaked Sam, amazed at how pitiful her own name could sound. "Emma's in the other bedroom. I can get her for you," she added lamely.

"We'll wait out here," said the voice.

The flashlight flicked off, the door swung closed, and Sam stumbled from the bed to grope for her robe on the nearby chair. Finding the robe and belting it snugly around her waist, she turned on the bedside lamp with a shaking hand. The antique-looking clock on the dresser said two-thirty. The police coming for Emma in the middle of the night could mean only one thing: somebody had died.

Gulping hard, Sam opened the door to find two men standing outside in the living room.

"I'm terribly sorry to disturb you, Miss Bridges. I'm Arthur Conland, the night manager, and this is Officer Peterson."

"Jimmy Peterson," said the policeman, giving Sam an apologetic smile. Jimmy Peterson was young, with a square, clean-shaven face, short blond hair, and sincere blue eyes.

"As I said, we're sorry," repeated Conland, "but evidently the police received a message of great urgency from the governor's office in Atlanta. I'm afraid we'll need to see Miss Cresswell."

"I'll have to wake her up," said Sam, her teeth practically chattering with fear. "S-sit down."

Oh my God, poor Emma, Sam thought as the men settled onto a sofa in the suite's spacious living area. Her knees felt weak. This was really happening! The police showing up in the middle of the night! She nearly stumbled climbing the three short steps to Emma's room.

Sam pushed open the door. The room was awash with the blue-white glow of the television and the sound of an old shoot-'em-up western. Emma slept soundly, looking like a child in her sleep.

After muting the sound on the TV, Sam gave Emma's shoulder a gentle shake.

"Emma."

Emma cocked open one eye.

"Emma, the police are here."

The eye closed. Emma turned on her side, mumbling sleepily, "Sam, that isn't funny."

"They really are. I mean it."

It took Sam a couple more tries to convince Emma she had to get out of bed. Finally, with a ragged sigh of exasperation, Emma pulled on her robe and marched into the living room.

"What's the problem, officer?" she asked regally.

"Miss Emma Cresswell?"

"I'm Emma Cresswell."

"Could I see some identification, please, Miss Cresswell?"

"Would you mind telling me exactly what this is all about?"

The officer was now turning his hat round and round in his hands. "Ma'am, my name is Officer Peterson, with the city police here in Savannah. We had a call tonight from the governor's office, saying your father had called them and was distraught over the possibility that something might have happened to you. He asked that we verify your whereabouts."

"Excuse me," Emma said, raising one eyebrow, "but that doesn't sound like my father."

"Brent Cresswell was the name we got, ma'am. Evidently the credit card center called him to verify a lost or stolen card report, and he feared for your well-being."

"That is the most ridiculous thing I have ever heard," snapped Emma. "My father has never in his life even *wondered* about my well-being!" Even as she said it, she remembered her father's desire to stay in closer touch from now on.

Could that be it? Could he really be concerned about her because she'd reported the credit card lost? But then Emma had a terrible thought: *He didn't do this because he cares about me. He did it because he's just afraid I'll vanish from the face of the earth before he can find a way to use me against Mother!*

"We couldn't very well ignore a request from the governor's office, ma'am," explained the policeman.

"Officer Peterson, I am eighteen years of age

and no longer a minor. I see this as a violation of my privacy, and—"

"Please, Miss Cresswell, if you'll just show some identification, then me and Mr. Conland here can go back about our business, and you and your friend can go back to bed."

Sam thought the glare on Emma's expression could have stopped a speeding bullet. It was unbelievable. There Sam was, ready to die of fright, and Emma had this cop cowering in his boots. Sam was even beginning to feel a little sorry for Jimmy Peterson.

Without a word, Emma turned and swept into her room, returning a moment later with her wallet, which she virtually flung at Officer Peterson. After checking her driver's license, the two men apologized once more and left.

"I cannot believe what just happened," Emma said softly as soon as the girls were alone. She sank back into a chair.

"You were awesome!" Sam cried, her eyes shining.

"Thanks," Emma said in a monotone. But the look on Emma's face was not one of triumph. In fact, she looked terribly sad.

"I guess we should have called your father," offered Sam. "Parents do worry about these things."

"This little charade had nothing to do with worry," Emma replied with a sigh. "Believe me, I know the man. This was about power."

Sam, who wasn't sure she understood, had nothing to say.

"I can't think about it anymore," Emma added, turning to reenter her room. "Let's go back to bed and forget this ever happened."

The girls said good night and retired to their rooms. Sam fell immediately into a deep, dreamless sleep. But Emma's Technicolor dreams featured herself as a heroine, driving a beat-up VW bug on an urgent mission and leaving two evil hitchhikers behind in a cloud of dust. One looked vaguely like her father, and one was a blond-wigged Minnie Mouse waving a hand that sported an enormous diamond.

Much further north, in New Haven, Carrie looked up from the political science textbook and rubbed her eyes. She'd have to get some sleep soon if she expected to do well on her midterm exam the next day. She found herself thinking that if the night had gone as she'd planned, she wouldn't still be cramming here at three in the morning. Fighting a rising irritation with Josh, she opened her desk drawer to find one of the candy bars she kept hidden there.

They had met at eight o'clock in Josh's room to study together for the test. But Josh, who wasn't as far behind in his work as she was, had wanted to talk. The talk had soon escalated into an argument, eclipsing any possibility of study.

"I think I've been pretty patient, if you want to

know the truth," Josh had said after bringing up the subject of spring break.

"You have been," Carrie had meekly agreed.

The fact that she was spending spring break with Billy had been eating at him, she knew. But she had been so busy! She hadn't seen much of Josh lately; when she did, she'd been so rushed that it was easy to avoid the issue. A little guiltily, Carrie realized that she had hoped to sidestep it entirely. Anyway, she would be spending time with Sam and Emma, too. It wasn't *just* Billy.

"So listen, we've got to deal with this," Josh had pressed.

Carrie had tapped her pen lightly on the notes they were starting to review. "We're watching the Third Reich come to power, and you're worried about spring break?" she had joked, trying to bring Josh back to the classwork.

Josh had grabbed the pen from her hand and in his frustration had sent it flying across the room.

"I'm sick of this, Carrie!" he had exploded. "We never talk anymore! You're always at the newspaper, or at the library, or in the darkroom, or in New York . . . when are you going to have some time for me? Or is that just not enough of a priority anymore?"

"I do care about you, Josh, it's just that—"

"It's just that you're planning to spend the only free time you've had all year with someone else."

"Josh, I've admitted I'm confused . . ."

"Well, I'm confused, too. I'm confused about

how some guy from last summer could have made such an impression that you'd throw away a five-year relationship!"

Carrie had looked in silence at her hands, waiting to see if his anger was spent. She still loved him so much. Why couldn't he understand that it was just different now? "Josh, I—" she started.

"No, wait," Josh had interrupted. He'd lowered his voice, and Carrie noted a new, serious tone.

"The fact is," he had continued, "since you don't seem willing to do anything about it, I'm going to call the shots. I know you've been planning this trip for a long time, and I wouldn't ask you to call it off. But if you're still confused when you get back, I'm ready to start seeing someone else."

Carrie had felt something catch in her throat.

"Someone in particular?" she had ventured, and was stunned to see Josh fighting a guilty smile as his face flushed all the way up to his hairline.

"Well, there's someone I'm attracted to."

Oh my God, it's Sarah Lovett! Carrie had thought, now feeling she'd completely misinterpreted the secretive smiles they'd exchanged passing in the hall. White-hot jealousy seared like molten lava through her veins. *How dare she?* Carrie had thought.

"Josh," she had managed to strangle out, "please don't ever think you don't mean the world to me. I guess I've just been so busy that I didn't see how unfair this has been to you."

In the silence that had ensued, Josh had reached for her hand, holding it tightly between both of his, and finally raising it to his lips for a kiss. He had given out with a heart-rending "Oh, Carrie" before taking her into his arms.

Fear of losing him had sweetened the moment, and quickly renewed her attraction to him. Josh had kissed her passionately, and Carrie, returning the kiss, had felt an overwhelming desire for him. He had been her first love. . . .

What am I doing? Carrie had found the presence of mind to ask herself. A moment later, she had gently disengaged herself from Josh's embrace. Josh had pounded his fist on the wall in frustration.

"How do you think this makes me feel?" he had cried. "You're spending your only vacation with that guy, and I'm not even allowed to touch you!"

Josh had rushed from the room, slamming the door on his way out. When he hadn't returned after fifteen minutes, Carrie had gone back to her dorm. That had been hours ago. He hadn't called.

Now, with another half-hour of study facing her, Carrie couldn't see that anything positive had been accomplished. She was insecure about Josh's feelings for her, guilty about spring break, and even a little guilty about her passionate response to Josh, considering she was seeing Billy in less than a week. To top it off, she probably wasn't going to ace this test the next day.

Finishing her candy bar, she reached into the drawer for another. At least she no longer had to worry about her eating habits adding unwanted pounds to her figure.

She knew what to do about that.

Over breakfast in the quaint tearoom, Sam promised herself she'd have a talk with Emma. After all, she was not the type of babe who beat around the bush. If Emma was drinking too much, then they should talk about it. That's what real friends were for.

But Emma got there first.

"Listen, Sam, I think you'll be happy to know I've turned over a new leaf, so to speak," Emma said as she pushed her serrated spoon into a section of grapefruit. "You were right when you said my family's driving me crazy, and I want you to know I'm finished with all that."

"Emma, it's not just your family, it's, well . . ."

"I know. I'm taking my share of blame here and now. I've been so self-absorbed lately! I'm sure I can't be much fun to be around."

"No, no," Sam protested. Somehow the conversation was getting away from Emma's drinking, which Sam had been working up the courage to ask her about.

"You know I really admire you, Sam," Emma continued.

"Me?" Sam squeaked.

"You!" Emma affirmed. "You aren't afraid to

get out there and take chances! You have an idea of what you want, and you go after it."

"Well, I try to," Sam began. "I mean—"

"Take your job, for instance," Emma continued earnestly. "Dancing at Disney World. How many girls do you think dream of that? And you're doing it!"

"I, uh . . ." Sam stammered.

"I want to be more daring, like you are," Emma said.

Okay, Sam, here's your chance, she said to herself. *Just open your mouth and tell Emma the truth.* But somehow her mouth wouldn't open. She just kept stirring extra sugar into her coffee.

"I feel like I've never done anything really adventurous in my whole life," Emma continued.

"But you've been all over the world!" said Sam.

"Yes, I have. With my nannies and my chauffeurs, in my family's private jet, with a wall of money and influential people shielding me from making any decisions on my own."

"You made your own decision to be an au pair last summer," countered Sam, "and your family didn't get you that job. You jumped right in and snagged it yourself."

"But look at the kind of job it was, Sam. In a beautiful place full of wealthy people, enjoying a wonderful, secure position with Jeff and Jane Hewitt, the world's most loving family. Where's the adventure in that? It was more like I traded one kind of palace for another."

"Your sailing abilities saved our butts last Christmas," Sam reminded her.

"That was an accident. I'm talking about the courage to make a plan. I'll bet you've already decided on your next step after Disney World."

Tell her! Tell her! the voice screamed inside of Sam. It looked like time for both of them to own up to things. Unfortunately, Sam was enjoying Emma's admiration of her too much to confess the truth. She just couldn't bear the thought of how Emma would look at her after she knew Sam was nothing more than a waitress at a third-rate steak house.

Sam sat up a little straighter and flung her hair back over her shoulders. "As a matter of fact, I do," Sam said coolly. "I'm going to be an actress."

"See?" Emma said emphatically. "I keep feeling like I want to step through the looking glass, and you're already there."

This was going entirely too far. "Emma, listen, it's not really like that—" Sam ventured. But before she could continue, she was interrupted.

"Howdy, ladies," came a familiar voice from above their seats. Looking up, the girls saw Jimmy Peterson, now in street clothes, holding two red roses in his hand.

"Thought I'd drop by to apologize again for last night. I don't make a habit of disturbing the rest of pretty young ladies. Or at least if I do, I try to make it a pleasant experience," said Jimmy, handing Sam and Emma each a rose.

"Why, thank you," said Emma.

"That is so thoughtful. I can't believe it," crooned Sam.

"I'd be happy to show you Savannah if you want to stick around. I mean, I understand you've got to be headin' north an' all. I just thought—"

"Wait a minute," said Emma, shifting her attention from the delicate scent of the rose she held. "How did you know we were heading north?"

"I'd imagine every cop along I-95 knows you're headin' north," Jimmy answered, leaning on the coatrack next to Sam. "One of my buddies from the station moonlights as security at one of the hotels over on Hilton Head, and he said an alert was issued last night from the governor of South Carolina, too. You must be one special young lady to have every governor on the Eastern seaboard watchin' after you."

"Thank you, Jimmy," said Emma, twirling the rose in her fingers. "You've been kinder than you'll ever know. And thank you for the invitation. We really can't stay, though."

"Think nothin' of it. Y'all come back to Savannah one day, hear?"

With a slight tip of his head, Jimmy Peterson turned and made his way from the tearoom. Sam watched Emma, waiting for her response.

Emma studied the petals of the rose in her hands. She was remembering her still-vivid dream of the night before. *I'm tired of not being the person I want to be! I'm tired of feeling smothered by my family!* she thought. There was absolutely no reason why her father should know her route and keep tabs on exactly where she was every minute of this trip.

"So, Sam," she said casually, looking up with a mischievous gleam in her eye, "still want to go to the mountains?"

SEVEN

With the sun shining warmly into the interior of the Sunbird and the South Carolina pines scenting the spring air, Carrie and Emma glided along the picturesque two-lane road. They'd chosen to stay off the highway for this first leg of their new route north. Passing through the countryside and quaint small towns made them feel they were definitely off the beaten path.

"I love this!" Sam yelled into the wind, "I feel so . . . so . . . what's the word for this, Emma?"

"Euphoric!" Emma sang out.

"Right, euphoric!" Sam echoed. She threw her arms behind her head and closed her eyes blissfully. "Ah, the lure of the open road! No wonder so many songs and stories are written about this. It's almost as good as falling madly in love with some incredibly gorgeous guy."

Just then a billboard featuring a giant ice cream cone dipped in chocolate caught Sam's eye. "Hey, Em, there's Dairy Dip a mile ahead. Can we stop? Please please please please?"

"We just ate breakfast a couple of hours ago!"

"So? Fresh air makes me hungry!" Sam responded reasonably.

A minute later, Emma gave in and turned into a small gravel lot beside a white-painted stand topped by a human-sized statue of an ice cream cone with a cute little swirl on the top. The menu, displayed in colorful pictures above the counter, offered everything from foot-long hot dogs to banana splits.

"Maybe I'll have the chili instead," Sam vacillated.

"It's real good chili," said the girl behind the window. Sam read "Kelly" off her nametag. She looked younger than she and Emma, Sam noted. *Shades of Big Al's*, she thought. She shook off the feeling and asked, "How 'bout the Strawberry-Butterscotch Extravaganza?"

"That's good, too," said Kelly.

"Sam, would you please make up your mind?" said Emma.

"Okay, okay," Sam said, then leaned in to give her order to Kelly. "I'll have a chili dog deluxe *and* a hot fudge sundae supreme," she said.

"Yuck!" Emma said, wrinkling her nose in distaste.

"And another chili dog deluxe for my friend here," Sam added.

"Sam," Emma protested, "I don't want a chili dog."

Sam turned to look at her. "Have you ever had a chili dog?"

96

"Well, no," Emma began.

"Then how do you know you don't want one?" Sam asked reasonably. She turned to the young girl behind the counter. "You tell her, Kelly. They're good, aren't they?"

"The best," Kelly agreed.

"I rest my case," Sam said solemnly, folding her arms.

Emma looked from Kelly to Sam and back to Kelly again, who stood there patiently, waiting to put the order in.

Emma had to laugh. "Fine. I'll eat a chili dog."

A few minutes later, Kelly slid the two chili dogs through the slide-up screen and stared anxiously at Emma as she picked up the chili dog. Emma regarded the paper-wrapped concoction doubtfully. Finally she reached out tentatively to gingerly lift one corner of the wrapping.

"Don't look at it," Sam advised her. "Just open your mouth, shove it in, and chew. Think of this as an initiation into your new life."

Sam's last words triggered a response. *After all*, Emma reasoned, *I've eaten all kinds of exotic foods in other countries*. South Carolina, at the moment, was seeming somewhat like another country to Emma. In one swift move she unwrapped the dog and took her first bite.

"So?" asked Sam. She and Kelly stood waiting for Emma's reaction.

Emma grinned. "This is actually not bad," she replied, folding back the wrapping some more and taking another bite. "Not bad at all."

"Welcome to America," said Sam.

Emma laughed, and she and Sam raced to finish off their chili dogs. Then Sam got her sundae and the two girls sat at one of the picnic tables located in a shady area on the side of the Dairy Dip.

As Emma watched Sam slurp the sundae into her mouth, she realized she felt something she hadn't felt in a long time—completely happy. She raised her legs up onto the bench and clasped her hands around her knees, lifting her head to the sun. Suddenly, everything felt right. Even the worn denim of her jeans felt perfect under her fingers. Just that morning Emma had dug into the bottom of her suitcase to find the faded jeans she had worn last summer on Sunset Island. She'd barely worn them since, but now that they were on her again, it felt like being with an old friend.

Memories flooded back, starting with when she'd first bought them to help bring her wardrobe more in line with what the other girls were wearing. Walks on the beach with Kurt, happy casual evenings with the Hewitt family, free afternoons and evenings at the Play Café with her new friends Carrie and Sam—these jeans had seen it all. How could she have let them languish, neatly folded and unworn, for so long?

"Yum, I could eat another," Sam said, licking up the last bite of melted ice cream.

"So eat another, then," Emma said.

Sam stared at her. "Where's the wrinkled

nose? The air of disdain? I mean, I cultivate at least half of my gross eating habits just so I can get a rise out of you!"

Emma laughed and stood up to stretch. "Who cares? This is the new anything-goes Emma."

Sam threw the plastic sundae dish into a trash can and licked some chocolate off her finger. "What happened to the old uptight-heiress Emma?"

"I have banished her for the duration," Emma said regally as they headed toward the car.

"Oh, I see," Sam said in the same tone of voice as Emma. As they passed the order window she turned to wave at Kelly. "Do tender our compliments to the chef!" she called.

Kelly grinned hospitably. "Anytime. Y'all come back, now."

The girls had rounded the corner and started the car when Kelly called after them, "Hey, the radio says there's a powerful big storm coming in from the west. Y'all drive careful!"

But it was Sam's turn to drive, and with Graham Perry's latest tape blasting from the stereo, neither Sam nor Emma heard Kelly's warning. Both girls waved cheerily as the car kicked up gravel and hit the open road.

"Hi, this is Carrie, and I can't take your call right now . . ."

Carrie lunged for the phone. "I'm here, I'm here, just a minute while I turn off this stupid machine."

She had heard the phone on her way up the

stairs, and for some reason had felt it was a call she needed to catch. Flicking off the answering machine, she spoke again into the handset. "Hello?"

"So rumor has it I'm talking to an actual person," came a deep male voice.

"Billy!" Carrie breathed into the phone. "I just had a feeling . . . I'm so glad it's you." Carrie sat down on the bed, cradling the phone receiver with her shoulder.

"As Pres would say, you're a hard dog to keep under the porch, you know that?" Pres, the bass player for Flirting with Danger, was from Tennessee, and the other guys in the band were always quoting his colorful Southern expressions.

"That's cuz this dog works like one," Carrie quipped. "I'm hardly ever in my room."

"So I've discovered," Billy said. "So how's life in the fast lane?"

"Exhausting," Carrie replied truthfully. "I just came back from a midterm."

"No doubt a piece of cake for you, oh brainy one," Billy said lightly.

"I wish," Carrie said. The truth was that her midterm in English Lit really had been difficult. And Josh, who had sat only two rows away, wouldn't even look at her, let alone speak. But all that seemed so much less important now.

"So, listen, I've got a surprise for you," Billy continued.

"You're flying to Yale to whisk me off to Paris for a few days before we all meet at Sunset Island?" Carrie guessed hopefully.

"Sorry, not that good," Billy said with a laugh. "Someday, though . . . anyway, here's the deal. The band's booked at the Play Café the first night you're back on the island."

"Hey, that's great!" Carrie exclaimed. "I'd love to hear the Flirts again. But how did that happen? I thought it was off season. They don't usually have bands at the café in April, do they?"

"True, and they don't usually have fires, either. But they did a couple of weeks ago," Billy reported.

"At the Play Café?" Carrie asked with concern. "Was anyone hurt?"

"Fortunately not," Billy told her. "The way I understand it, some wires got crossed in the heating system. The clean-up is just about finished, but the kitchen's pretty much of a loss. We're doing a benefit to help Ken get the place put back together in time for summer."

"Ken must be devastated!" Carrie exclaimed. Ken Miner, who owned the Play Café, was a favorite with all his patrons.

"He's holding up pretty well, but the bank that holds the mortgage on the place is hurting. That building's mostly wood, you know. You can only get so much fire insurance on a structure like that, and the most expensive stuff—all that equipment—was in the kitchen."

"Wait a minute," said Carrie. "How big a benefit can you pull off when hardly anyone's around at this time of year?"

"Hey, I told you the Flirts have been gaining

101

quite a following around the colleges in Portland, Bangor, even down through New Hampshire and as far away as Boston now. Plenty of kids can't afford to go too far for spring break—they'll spend a Saturday night on Sunset for a good cause, no problem."

"I can't wait," Carrie said, smiling wistfully. She wished she could make the time between now and leaving for Sunset Island a mere millisecond. "I'm so excited!"

Billy laughed. "I'll see to that."

Carrie was glad a blush couldn't be seen over the phone. A thought popped into her mind: that was the difference between Josh and Billy. Billy could actually make her blush.

"So listen," Billy continued, "say hi to Emma and Sam for me. And speaking of Sam, Pres is watching the horizon for the first sign of that wild red hair of hers. What's the deal with her, anyway?"

"Last I heard, she was footloose and fancy-free," said Carrie. "But that was over a week ago, and you know how it goes."

"I do know how it goes," said Billy softly, "and I hope you're willing to wait another week for me."

"Don't even consider another possibility," Carrie answered fervently. "I'm not." Oh, she was so thankful she'd had her wits about her last night!

"Okay then, gotta run. You have a safe trip."

Carrie told Billy good-bye, hung up, and flopped on the bed. She was exhausted from staying up all night, but now her tiredness had a pleasant glow to it. Just a few more days, and she'd be with Billy!

All her efforts of the past couple of weeks were coming to a satisfying conclusion now: midterms would be over, and even the paper would shut down for spring break. As to her other new pastime, she knew she was pushing it, forcing herself to vomit after meals now as well as after between-meal indulgences. But it was working so well that she was hopeful a change in her appearance would be apparent by spring break after all.

She'd already lost almost five pounds.

"So what about Pres?" Emma asked Sam. They were now about an hour past Columbia, South Carolina, where they'd gotten on a small highway. The landscape had turned from pine flats to soft, rolling hills.

"What about him?" said Sam.

"Aren't you excited about seeing him?"

"Well, yeah. In a way. I guess."

"Very decisive answer, Sam." Emma laughed.

Sam swept a strand of hair out of her eyes and reached over to insert another tape into the tape deck.

"He's . . . I don't know," Sam said lamely. "I mean, he's gorgeous. And exciting. And hot . . ."

"You poor baby!" Emma teased. "How can you stand him, then?"

Sam sighed. "It's just not . . . I don't know. It's not love."

"So what's love, then?" Emma asked.

"How am I supposed to know?" Sam said. "I've never been in it. But when I am in it, I'll know. You know?"

"I suppose I do," Emma said thoughtfully, turning down the music so they could hear each other better. "I mean, before Kurt I didn't know what love was, either."

"But now that you're in it, you know, right?" Sam asked. "So I rest my case."

Emma nodded thoughtfully. "I guess if you don't feel that way about Pres, then you don't, no matter how hot he is."

"I just have this feeling that love should be . . . gut-wrenching or something," Sam said passionately. "Like all you can do is think about that person. You can't eat, you can't sleep, that sort of thing."

"That's how I felt with Kurt last summer," Emma said. "It wasn't always so wonderful, though."

"I don't know," Sam sighed. "Maybe it's not all it's cracked up to be. Or maybe I'm missing some love chromosome or something. I don't know if I'll ever . . ." Sam paused and squinted into the distance. "Hey, Em, are those the mountains?"

Emma, who'd been keeping her eyes on the road, checked the horizon. A dark, peaked mass to the west seemed to stretch from north to south.

"That can't be the mountains yet," she answered. "We're still hours away from Asheville."

"Well, it sure looks like something."

"I hate to say this, but what it looks like is clouds. Lots of clouds. I think we're headed into a storm." For the first time, Emma noticed what her eyes had been observing but her mind hadn't registered. A number of cars coming the other way on the highway had their lights on, although it was sunny, warm, and only three-thirty in the afternoon.

"We'd better find a place to pull over and put the top up," Emma said.

Setting the emergency blinkers to flash, she pulled off onto the shoulder at the next straightaway. Opening the latches at the top of the windshield in preparation for contact, she pressed the button to raise the top.

There was a muted groan, followed by nothing.

"What's going on?" asked Sam over the wind. Now that they were stopped, it was evident that the breeze blowing through the car hadn't just been due to their speed on the highway.

"I don't know. I'm doing the same thing I've always done," Emma said, trying the button again. This time she didn't even get the muted groan. Nothing happened at all.

"I think we'd better get off the highway," said Sam, nervously eyeing the traffic whizzing by them. "We might need help, and it's a cinch we're not going to find a mechanic sitting out here."

Quickly they climbed into the car and merged back into traffic. The sun was now behind the clouds, and the air itself seemed to have a heavy, greenish cast. They passed a truck whose driver honked, pointed ahead, and rippled his fingers downward in an imitation of rain.

"We know!" mouthed Sam, with a gesture of helplessness.

A car full of guys passed on their left. The rear window rolled down and a cute blond-haired guy stuck his head out. "Hey, storm!" he called out, pointing deliberately into the distance.

"We know!" Emma mouthed, rolling her eyes. "They must think we're crazy!" she yelled to Sam.

"We probably are," Sam answered. "We're driving into a storm with the top down!"

The next exit had the unlikely name of Boomer, but beggars couldn't be choosers. Once off the highway, they were dismayed to find a sign that read: Boomer, 5 Miles.

"Maybe we'll get there ahead of the storm," Emma said hopefully.

Sam eyed the rapidly darkening skies. "Well, at least we're off the highway," she muttered. "Now it won't be so bad."

The words were no sooner out of her mouth than the sky opened. Rain poured down in curtains, sweeping over the car and soaking Sam and Emma within seconds. Both of them shrieked at the first sensation of cold water drenching their hair and clothes, but it was immediately obvious there was nothing they could do. It was hard to see and they couldn't drive very quickly. From time to time, Emma tried the button that raised the top, but by then she really didn't expect anything to happen.

After what Sam thought must have been the longest few minutes of her life, they came to a crossroads with a few buildings scattered about the intersection. Fortunately one of the nearest said Sonny's Gas and Garage.

A rippled metal roof sheltered the area between the station's glass window and the pumps. Emma pulled in under it and stopped the car. She and Sam turned to regard each other.

"You should see yourself!" Sam gasped with laughter, pointing at Emma.

Emma's hair was plastered to her skull on one side, and formed a slick lopsided peak on the other. She looked like a conehead experiencing slippage.

"I can't believe I could look any funnier than you do," Emma replied before dissolving into a fit of giggles.

Sam twisted the rearview mirror to get a look at herself. Her mascara ran in rivulets down her face. The lines ran all around her mouth and met below her chin, giving her a painted Fu Manchu–style beard. "Whoa, what a babe!" she shrieked. "All I can say is, I'm glad there are no cute guys here to see me looking like this!" She looked up. "Uh-oh," she said. "Cancel that thought."

Two guys had just pushed open the door of the gas station and were headed over to them.

"I am *totally* humiliated," Sam lamented. "And they're cute, too."

The guys peered at the girls, then at the flooded convertible, with amused faces. Already the sudden downpour was slowing to a trickle.

The muscular, sandy-haired one could barely control his mirth. "Hey, gals!" he said. "I see you've been out enjoyin' some fresh air on this beautiful day."

"Oh, funny," Sam commented coolly, going for a sassy shake of her hair. *Oops*. Her hair was plastered to her head. The move came off as more of a tic.

The other guy opened Emma's door for her. She found herself looking into his vivid blue eyes. "Everyone out of the pool!" he called as a flood of water sloshed out onto the ground.

"We couldn't get the top to go up," Emma blurted out. She slid out of the driver's seat.

"Really?" said the sandy-haired guy. "We thought maybe this was a mobile wet T-shirt party."

Sam slipped out of her seat and stood next to him. With her cowboy boots (which squished a bit) she was a little taller than the guy. She gave him a look of intense interest. "Let me ask you a question," she said, cocking her head to the side. "Has anybody ever told you you should be a stand-up comic?"

The guy looked very flattered. "No, but I surely have thought about it," he said seriously.

"Well," Sam answered solemnly, "don't."

The guy turned a bright shade of red.

"She's just a little testy because of our predicament," Emma interrupted hastily. "Right, Sam?"

Sam didn't answer. She was too busy looking haughty.

"Listen, is there anyone who could look at the car to see if the top can be fixed?" Emma asked the guys.

"Also dry clothes would be a happening event," Sam added, careful not to include the sandy-haired guy in her gaze. "Is there somewhere we can change?"

The dark-haired guy with the beautiful blue eyes gave them a friendly smile and said, "You sure picked the right place to stop. Sonny's just down the road at Ma's, and he's the best mechanic for a hundred miles. Why don't you grab your stuff and let us run you over there? You can change, talk to Sonny, and get some of the best catfish in the country while he checks your car."

Catfish? "That would be lovely," Emma said with her most well-bred smile.

When the guys had gone around the side of the station, Emma turned on Sam. "Why were you so rude to that guy?" she demanded.

Sam grabbed Emma's arm. "Did you see how cute he is? I'm dying!"

"What are you talking about? The short one that you were so mean to?"

"Those muscles!" Sam rhapsodized. "Believe me, rude works. I look like the Swamp Thing at the moment. I had to do something to get his attention!"

Emma shook her head. "Sometimes I think you are completely certifiable."

Just then the guys pulled up in a red pickup truck. The girls threw their stuff under a tarp in back and then squeezed into the cab with them.

The guys introduced themselves as Jake (the dark-haired one) and Scott (with the sandy hair). They were down from Knoxville to participate in a customized-sports car rally in the area. They knew Sonny through a mutual passion for car racing. Jake explained that they usually towed their race car on a trailer behind the truck, but right now it was inside Sonny's garage for a final tuneup.

"Thanks a lot," Emma said, climbing as daintily from the truck as possible.

"Listen," Scott said, sticking his head out of the window, "if you're still around in a couple of hours, there's a twilight bluegrass jam here at Ma's. Either of you gals clog?"

Clog. It seemed to be a verb of some sort, but Emma hadn't a clue what it meant. "I don't know what—" Emma began.

"Do we clog?" Sam broke in. "Is the Pope Catholic?"

"Swell!" Scott said, his face breaking into a huge grin.

"But I—" Emma tried again.

"Okay, okay," Sam interrupted Emma again. "I'll tell the truth."

"Thank you," Emma said with dignity.

"The truth is, I'm only fair, but Emma here is a national champion!"

"Get out of town!" Jake crowed.

"How's about y'all have an early dinner, and warm up your tootsies, and we'll be back here when the garage closes?" Scott asked eagerly.

"What have you gotten me into now?" Emma demanded as the guys drove away and Sam hustled her into the restaurant.

"Just a little dancing," Sam said innocently.

"Dancing I have no idea how to do," Emma said as they pushed through the door into the ladies' room.

"Hey, where's the new, adventurous, free-spirited Emma?" Sam asked, rummaging through her suitcase for the perfect clogging outfit.

"Maybe I could learn to clog," Emma allowed, "but you just told them I was a champion!"

"Emma, Emma, Emma, what's a little hyperbole between friends?" Sam asked, semidistractedly as she pawed through her clothes. "Aha!" she crowed. She held up a metallic bra top with coins dangling from the bottom and smiled wickedly. "Just wait until Scott sees the real me."

"Is that the kind of thing a person wears clogging?" Emma asked uncertainly.

"Sure," Sam said. "In fact, a real champion like you would dress even trashier. Cloggers are known for their sexy outfits." She gave Emma a wicked smile. "Time for your transformation!"

EIGHT

When the girls came out of the ladies' room, Emma still wasn't certain that either of them had made the right choice for clogging outfits. Sam was wearing the metallic bra top with a micro-miniskirt made out of metallic mesh. Her red cowboy boots (which she had dried with her hair dryer) completed the outfit. Sam had dressed Emma in a sheer black shirt with bright flowers covering her breasts, and a hot pink stretchy miniskirt that Emma kept pulling self-consciously away from the curve of her butt. It was totally unlike the clothes Emma usually wore. But Sam had convinced her to take a chance, and had used words like *stuffy* and *boring* and *heiress*. Somehow Emma had gone along with it, and here she was, sidling into the restaurant, feeling like a total idiot.

Fortunately there weren't too many patrons to witness Emma's embarrassment. In fact there was only one, the infamous Sonny, and he was impossible to miss. He was one of the largest human beings Emma and Sam had ever seen. It wasn't that Sonny was fat; he was just . . . big. His boyish moon-sized face wore a friendly smile as the girls introduced themselves, but took on a solemn expression as they explained the problem with Emma's car.

"Wayl, I dunno. Them new-fangled cars kin be right tetchy t' mess with," he drawled. "On t' other hand, might jes' be a li'l bug needs workin' out." Heaving his massive frame out of the booth, he continued, "I'll jes' have me a look-see, and git back to ya . . . y'all gonna be right heah?"

Emma and Sam looked at each other—where else could they go?

"Fine," Emma said. "And I can pay you by cash or traveler's check, if you prefer it to a credit card," she added.

"That'd be jes' fine, ma'am," Sonny said, ambling toward the door. He turned back to them and bucked his head toward the floor shyly. "That's mighty purty stuff you'uns got on," he added, then went through the door.

"Told you," Sam said with her chin up. She headed for the jukebox, which featured mostly country artists. The only ones Sam knew were Elvis Presley and Garth Brooks, so that's what she played.

Emma and Sam slid into a booth to the strains of "Heartbreak Hotel." Sam let her foot dangle off the edge of the seat and admired her newly dry cowboy boots.

"I would have had a coronary if these boots got ruined," Sam said.

"It's amazing that you found another pair," Emma said, unsuccessfully attempting to lengthen her tiny mini skirt. "They're almost exactly like the ones that got wrecked when we were lost at sea."

"I know," Sam agreed. "I felt positively superstitious until I had them back on my feet." She wriggled her toes blissfully.

"'Scuse me, but no legs up on the upholstery," came a female voice so deep and raspy that it sounded as if the speaker were in the bottom of a well.

Sam and Emma looked up at a female version of Sonny. She was six feet tall, well over two hundred solid pounds, with steel-gray hair and arms the size of tree trunks. The woman's mouth was wrapped around a filterless cigarette.

"I'm Ma," the voice boomed. Ma looked over their outfits with obvious disdain. "Will y'all be orderin'?"

"Hot chocolate?" Sam asked.

"I'll have tea," Emma added meekly, again attempting to adjust her skirt.

"Hmph," was Ma's reply as she turned away.

"I'm changing," Emma hissed as she began to slide out of the booth. "This outfit is tacky."

"Well, thank you very much, Miss Heiress," Sam said in a hurt voice. "That happens to be one of my favorite outfits."

"I'm sorry, Sam," Emma said. "I didn't mean anything by it. I mean—"

"Look, it's nothing to me if you don't want to wear it," Sam said, but Emma could tell how hurt she really was.

"I'll . . . I'll keep it on," Emma said, sliding back into the booth. "Probably it's just that I'm not used to it, right?"

Ma sat the tea and hot chocolate down on the table before Sam could answer Emma.

"Kitchen opens in five minutes," came Ma's huge, gravelly voice. "Catfish platter comes with your catfish, your homefries, and your slaw. Catfish dinner includes that plus your choice of two from your green beans, your white beans, your turnip greens, and your hush puppies. Will you *ladies* be wantin' to order?"

Emma wasn't too sure she liked the spin that Ma put on the word *ladies*, but figured it might just be her imagination. Sam hadn't even noticed. She was too busy reveling in the joys of a down-home catfish dinner.

"I'll have the dinner," Sam said promptly, "with green beans and extra hush puppies."

"Uh, the same," Emma said with what she hoped was a ladylike smile at Ma.

"Hmph," was Ma's reply as she trundled away toward the kitchen.

"Wow, a catfish dinner!" Sam exclaimed happily.

"I believe my father uses catfish as bait," Emma said, turning a little green.

"I wonder what a hush puppy is," Sam continued, ignoring Emma's comment.

Emma gulped. "I'm just hoping it doesn't involve an actual canine."

"Culinary adventure is a wonderful thing," Sam opined.

The door opened, and the first of the dinner customers started to filter into the restaurant.

"See?" Sam pointed out. "All the locals can't be wrong about *the* place to eat!"

As the restaurant filled up the girls noticed that several people had musical instruments with them, which they laid carefully on a chair or leaned against a wall.

"Catfish," Ma announced unceremoniously as she set the overloaded plates of food in front of them.

"Dig in!" Sam cried, and cut into the golden breaded fish.

Emma watched Sam with a look of trepidation on her face.

"What am I, the royal taster?" Sam asked around the food in her mouth. "Like if I die, you'll know not to chow down?"

Emma picked up her fork, delicately speared a piece of fish, and put it into her mouth.

"It's actually . . . good," she said finally.

"Two new foods in one day—oh, heart of mine, be still!" Sam laughed. She picked up a small fried blob. "By process of elimination, this must be the ole hush puppy." She bit into it. "It's bread. Fried

117

cornbread," Sam said with disappointment. "My mother makes fried cornbread."

"All of this is really very good!" Emma said with her mouth full. "If you don't mind eating fried, that is."

"Throw caution to the winds, live dangerously," Sam suggested.

They chewed happily for a while. Even Emma finished most of what was on her plate.

Finally Emma couldn't fit another morsel of food into her stomach. She daintily patted the side of her mouth with her napkin and asked Sam, "How long do you think we should wait before checking back with Sonny about the car?"

"Speak of the devil," Sam said, nodding toward the door of the restaurant, where Sonny, Jake, and Scott had just entered. "Ask him now, if you want."

The three guys waved to Ma, smiled at Sam and Emma, and took a booth near the door. Ma immediately sashayed over with three steaming plates, as if she'd been waiting for them.

"On second thought," said Sam, "maybe you'd better wait till after they eat."

Emma was feeling a bit uneasy. If her car was ready, why wasn't Sonny presenting a bill? Of course, if it was a major problem, maybe he'd have to finish fixing it after dinner. A terrible thought crossed her mind: maybe the top couldn't be fixed and he just didn't want to tell her. She finally decided to be optimistic, and ordered an after-dinner cup of coffee. They were hours off their schedule, and would have to drive well into the night to reach Asheville.

Soon they heard the sound of stringed instruments being tuned. Sam and Emma watched as dinner tables were moved back against one wall to make room for a band and dance floor.

Sam was shifting in her seat, craning to see the table where Jake, Scott, and Sonny were now drinking coffee. She noticed Scott was doing the same thing in their direction.

"He's looking at me!" Sam whispered triumphantly to Emma.

"Of course he's looking at you," Emma said. "Everyone is looking at you. You're wearing a bra and mesh."

Sam flipped her hair back over her shoulder. "It was a fashion risk worth taking."

Suddenly the fiddle player got up, gave his instrument a quick tune, and started playing a merry, spirited bluegrass jig. Soon other players joined in, and the room swelled with music.

A number of people left their seats to join in an animated dance. Emma was fascinated. *So this is clogging!* she thought. The women, whose bodies hardly seemed to move at all, were beating out a rapid, complicated rhythm with their feet. The men did the same, but their steps were punctuated with occasional kicks, stomps, and something they did with their elbows that looked like a chicken flapping its wings. When the first song ended, Emma forced her attention back to the problem at hand.

"Listen, I don't want to be rude, but I really have to go ask Sonny about my car. I'm having an anxiety attack."

Emma strode purposefully to Sonny's side, where she had to lean close to his ear to make herself heard over the music.

"My car," she said with as much decorum as she could manage at this volume. "Were you able to fix it?"

"It wuz jes' like I figgered: a li'l belt come loose from the motor that runs yer top. Din' take but one li'l turn of a wrench, and she's good as new."

"That's wonderful! Let me get my wallet, and—"

"Fergit money," said Sonny, his eyes shining as he gave Emma another wink. "You know what I want."

Emma's heart thudded in her chest. "Ah, no. Not really . . ."

Sonny stood up, towering over Emma. She took a step back in fear. Surely somebody would help her. What was this giant going to try to do? "I want," he said in a low voice, "a dance."

Emma just stood there a moment. Then she remembered Sam's silly remark about her being a clogging champion. Jake and Scott must have told Sonny. *So that's it!*

"I'm sorry," Emma began graciously. "There appears to be a misunderstanding here—"

"Sonny told us he's not givin' your keys back until you dance with him," Jake said with a grin.

"Might as well not fight it," Scott added. "Sonny here is a dancin' fool."

Emma looked over at Sam, who was laughing so hard she could barely catch her breath. *No doubt about it*, Emma said to herself. *I am going to kill Sam, and then I'm making a run for it.*

"Look, Sonny, I'm sorry if—"

Emma never got to finish her statement. The next thing she knew, Sonny's massive arms were around her, her hand was in his bearlike paw, and she was being led into the dance.

Sonny, it turned out, was remarkably light on his feet. And even though Emma had not a clue as to how to do this kind of dancing, her early ballroom dance training at Madame Junot's in Lucerne held her in good stead. In other words, she knew how to follow.

The next half-hour passed in a blur of sound and motion. Emma had glimpses of Sam trading off dances with Jake and Scott, but she couldn't see much of anything around Sonny's five-acre chest. Sonny seemed determined not to relinquish her hand for even a moment, and the band moved from one song to another without pause.

Finally the band announced a break. Sonny let go of Emma just long enough to reach into his pocket. When he grasped her hand once again, it was to press her car keys gently into her palm.

"Hope I dint hold y'all up too long," he said with a sheepish grin. "But it shore was worth it!"

Sam and Emma paid their tab, made their good-byes to Jake, Scott, and Sonny, and didn't speak again until they were in the car and pulling out of Ma's lot.

"Yeow! Git right on it, li'l darlin'!" Sam hollered in an accurate impersonation of Sonny.

"I ought to kill you for pulling that stunt," Emma told Sam, but her voice told Sam that her heart wasn't really in the words.

"Come on, admit it," Sam wheedled, "you had fun."

"I did!" Emma laughed with delight. "I didn't even care after a while that this stupid skirt of yours rode up practically to my waist."

"Wait till Kurt sees the pictures I took," teased Sam. "I'll just innocently say that this is the guy Emma's been dating at school."

Emma laughed. "You're terrible!"

"I know, and you love it!" Sam crowed, cranking up the tunes on the radio.

Life with Sam is certainly never dull, Emma had to admit as she turned onto the highway for Asheville. She smiled to herself and headed toward the mountains.

Carrie was sorting laundry and planning to do a load of vacation clothes in the dorm's laundry room when a short tap on the door and a melodic voice calling her name announced Mona's presence in the hall outside.

"Ms. Carolyn Alden?" the voice inquired with mock formality. "I have a delivery here for you."

Carrie opened the door to find Mona practically hidden behind an enormous bouquet of long-stemmed red roses.

"For me?" she cried jubilantly. *That Billy!* she

thought to herself. *He's so impetuous with his money sometimes!*

"Who else?" asked Móna. "Or has Madonna been going around using your name again?"

Carrie took the vase and turned it from side to side, looking for the card.

"If you're looking for a card, don't bother," Mona continued. "And don't think I've taken on a new job delivering flowers, either. There's a gentleman waiting downstairs in the foyer. He looked so downhearted, I offered to run interference for him and bring them up myself."

Josh.

"Thanks, Mona," said Carrie, setting the flowers carefully in front of the mirror on her dresser. "Guess I'd better go down and talk to him."

"Whoa now—don't bowl anyone over with excitement or gratitude on your way down, okay?"

"Sorry, Mona. They're beautiful and everything, and you were sweet to bring them up. It's just that I'm not sure I'm looking forward to this conversation."

"I can dig that, girlfriend, but you could at least muster a smile. Those things aren't cheap, you know, and I think his heart's in the right place."

"That's what I'm afraid of," said Carrie, taking time for a heavy sigh before heading downstairs.

Josh was watching for her, and they saw each other the moment Carrie reached the foot of the stairs. Carrie was surprised at how the sight of him warmed her. It had been strange to feel so out of touch with him for the past couple of days, though she hadn't really acknowledged that until just this minute.

"Tell me I'm a jerk," Josh told Carrie sheepishly, his hands thrust into his pockets.

"You're not!" she protested.

"Yeah? I got so mad at you the other day, I stormed out of my own room," Josh retorted.

"That was kind of funny," Carrie said wryly.

"If you say you'll forgive me, I'll regain my sense of humor."

"Of course I do," Carrie insisted. "If you forgive me."

Josh's grin told her all she needed to know.

"The roses are so beautiful, Bil—" She had started to call him Billy! She couldn't believe it!

For a split second she thought maybe he hadn't noticed, but one look at his face showed her that he had.

"Even I don't deserve that," he said with a rueful attempt at a laugh.

Carrie felt tears welling up. "No, you don't," she said softly. *If only the earth would open up and swallow me right here and now!*

"Maybe I was hoping you'd had time to miss me and change your mind about this vacation." A moment ago, Josh's hands had been reaching out to hug her. Now his fingers were clenched into tight fists.

"No, Josh, really, I . . ." Carrie fumbled for the words that would make everything all right again, but no words came to her.

"Obviously, I'm just making an ass out of myself here," Josh said, trying for a lighthearted tone and failing miserably.

"No, Josh, I—"

"Yes," he corrected her. "It's my own fault. It's like I'm wearing a sign that says 'kick me.'"

"I'm sorry, really," Carrie, pleaded. "I didn't—"

"Just save it, Carrie, okay?" Josh said tersely. "Look, I'm willing to stand by what I told you. I'll give you till you get back from spring break but then you're going to have to choose."

"But I—"

"No more buts, Carrie," Josh interrupted. "It's him or me."

Tears were streaming down Carrie's face. She felt paralyzed.

"Good-bye, Carrie," Josh said, then turned and walked out the door.

By noon the next day, Emma and Sam were high in the Great Smoky Mountains. They had left the car in a lot at the foot of a hiking trail and carried a blanket and a picnic lunch up a winding mountain trail. Just as the park ranger had promised, the view from the ridge was spectacular. Sam inhaled deeply and flung her arms out wide as Emma took in the beauty of the mountain crests and valleys sprinkled with the delicate pink and white of dogwood blossoms. It occurred to Emma that she'd seen much more of the Swiss Alps than she ever had of her own country.

Sam and Emma spread their blanket near the

edge of a rocky cliff and sat back to feast their eyes, figuring they could wait a few minutes before digging into the carton of seafood salad (Emma's) and tuna sandwich with chips (Sam's) they'd procured at an Asheville delicatessen. It was then they heard the waterfall.

"Listen, Emma," said Sam, sitting up straight and cocking her head to locate the exact source of the sound. "I hear water. The map said there was a waterfall up here!"

With that, Sam grabbed her camera and scampered off to the right, disappearing over the edge of an outcropping of rock. A moment later her head popped back into view.

"C'mere, you won't believe this!" she called. Emma followed her to a rock ledge just on the other side of the ridge.

The falls were striking in their beauty, cascading down from the next ridge over, and creating a frothy, bubbling pool where they met the river below. A shimmering rainbow edged the mist surrounding them.

"Let's move our blanket down here!" exclaimed Sam. "There's room, and we'll have this view while we eat." Sam broke into one of her dance routine kicks and said, "If there were a couple of gorgeous mountain men around, I might even consider staying here forever!"

Emma started leading the way back up. When she saw their blanket, she stopped in her tracks. Someone in a fur coat was bending over to inspect what they were having for lunch. *How incredibly rude!* she thought. *That woman has the manners of a pig!* Suddenly it dawned on Emma: not pig, bear. The fur coat belonged to a bear. A large bear. And the bear had just lifted its snout to sniff out Emma's presence.

Emma stood stock still, completely paralyzed with fear. Dimly she remembered the ranger's warning at the entrance to the park: there were bears in the area. Well, it was a little too late now. She had no idea what to do.

"What's taking you so long?" Sam asked, coming up next to Emma. "I'm really starv—"

Emma grabbed Sam's arm in a vise-like grip and pointed mutely toward their blanket.

Sam was just as petrified as Emma. "We don't have bears in Kansas," she whispered weakly.

"Well, we sure don't have them on Beacon Hill!" Emma hissed.

The bear regarded the girls almost casually.

"Maybe it's like with a bee—you're not supposed to annoy him." She gulped.

A low growl rumbled up from the animal's chest.

"I think we're way past that stage," Emma whispered.

"Please go away, please go away, please go away," Sam chanted under her breath.

The growl grew to Richter-scale force, finally erupting from the bear's snarling mouth as an ear-splitting roar.

Without thinking, both girls ran for a nearby tree, where they crouched and cowered.

"What's he doing?" Sam said with her eyes shut tight.

"Eating," Emma said.

They kept themselves plastered to the tree, not daring to move for fear of angering the bear. It seemed like forever that they hid behind the slender safety of that tree.

"What was that?" asked Emma, in response to a particularly unpleasant sound.

"Bear belch," Sam reported.

When they looked again, the bear seemed to have settled in for a nap on the blanket. Any time one of the girls tried to move from her crouching position behind the tree, the bear snarled and made as if to lumber in their direction.

"What are we going to do, Em?" Sam whispered. "Aren't bears supposed to hibernate or something?"

"It's springtime!" Emma answered.

They waited there for what must have been forty-five minutes. As Emma tried to rub a cramp out of her leg, suddenly there came a deep rumble. It seemed to come from the air surrounding them.

"Please tell me that's not an entire herd of bears," Sam wailed softly.

"Pack," Emma said automatically. "And I think that was thunder. If you'll look to the west, I think you'll see the cause of it."

Beyond a ridge across the main valley, a dark cloud was advancing, and even as they watched, a fork of lightning streaked across it.

Great, thought Emma. *We're about to be caught in the rain for the second time in twenty-four hours.*

She found herself wishing with all her heart that the problem was as simple as being in her own little car with the top stuck down.

NINE

The next growl the girls heard was low, threatening, and constant. Too constant.

"It *is* a pack of bears!" Sam wailed, grabbing Emma. "This guy has brothers and sisters. We're dead meat!"

"No, it's a mechanical growl," Emma said, listening carefully. "You know, as in motor roar, not animal roar."

"As in maybe we're going to be saved?" Sam asked hopefully.

Together the girls crept to their lookout spot, slowly raising their heads so as not to attract the bear's attention. It didn't seem to matter, though. The bear had its back to them and appeared to be listening, too. But not for long. A forest-green Jeep suddenly appeared, churning through the woods, then fairly leaping into the clearing where the picnic blanket was spread. The bear didn't hang around to greet the new visitor, but galloped off at surprising speed and vanished into the trees.

Emma and Sam scrambled up from where they'd been trapped, lunchless, for over an hour now. The Jeep met them at their blanket. Behind the wheel was a uniform, and wearing the uniform was a rugged but gorgeous park ranger whose clothes did not disguise his perfect body. This was definitely not the meek-looking, balding ranger they'd talked to at the park entrance!

"I see you've met Tiger," said the man ruefully.

"Tiger didn't wait for a formal introduction," Sam said, looking toward the path along which Tiger had beat his hasty retreat.

The ranger laughed a friendly, booming laugh. "I'm Ted Ballinger, the guy who gets to go around apologizing for Tiger's rude manners."

Emma introduced the two of them. Sam was still busy watching to make sure Tiger wasn't on his way back for another visit.

"Don't worry," Ted told her. "He's scared to death of my Jeep. He won't come back."

"Thank God for small favors," Sam sighed with relief.

Finally she was able to turn her full attention to the magnificent specimen of guy-hood that stood before her. *Be still, my heart! This guy is hot.*

"The problem with Tiger is that he's been fed by so many tourists over the years, he's developed lousy manners. He doesn't seem interested in hurting anyone, but he's staged hostile take-overs of many a picnic basket," Ted explained.

He offered them a ride down the mountain.

They accepted gratefully. Sam was practically swooning in the Jeep's jumpseat, and she kept her eyes fixed on Ted as if she didn't want to miss the view for even a second.

"You girls stick around for another day or so, you might even see some snow," said the hunky-looking ranger. "That little shower on the next ridge is only the beginning—there's a major spring storm system heading this way."

"We're leaving tomorrow," said Emma. "We have to be in New York by Friday."

"Well, get out your boots and parkas," laughed Ted. "You're headed right for the brunt of the storm."

Ted saw them safely to their car, and waited as they started up and drove away.

"Now *that* is what I call adventure," Sam sighed. "Don't you think a park ranger would make a nice pet?"

Emma laughed. "You're incorrigble!"

Sam fluttered her eyelashes at Emma. "It's just part of my charm, ma'am, just part of my charm."

"Those buns!" Sam moaned. Ranger Ted was now almost two days behind them on the highway, and Sam had said the word *buns* in his memory at least fifteen times.

The previous day's drive to Washington on the Blue Ridge Parkway had been peaceful and scenic, with only a couple of patches of rain. But today, an icy wind had nipped at their cheeks as they packed the car. Now, as they headed toward New York City, the sky was low and blanketed by a thick gray mantle. Emma was concentrating seriously on her driving, but the heat inside the car was making Sam feel cozy enough to sleep.

"Mind if I have a little nap?"

"Not unless you're planning to drive at the same time" was Emma's reply.

"Oh, that famous Cresswell sense of humor," Sam remarked, settling in for a good sleep.

Emma drove for the next hour listening to classical music and daydreaming about Kurt. When she first saw the snowflakes, she reassured herself that they were just blowing around and didn't appear to be sticking.

But within a few miles the weather had changed drastically. The air was thick with whirling snow, and an icy layer of white had already started covering the road. Emma touched the brake pedal and felt the car fishtail. A tingle of fear ran up the back of her neck.

"Sam, wake up," Emma called to her.

"Wha—wha?" came Sam's sleepy voice from next to her.

"Wake up!" Emma commanded, using her best Katerina Cresswell voice. No one could sleep through that.

"What?" Sam said irritably, rubbing her eyes.

"It's snowing," said Emma, trying to stay calm as she wondered how she was going to pull over safely. Everyone was going so fast! Couldn't they see that the road was slick?

Sam sat up. "All right!" she cheered. It was the first snow she'd seen in a year. She'd forgotten how invigorating a good snowstorm could be.

"Sam, I mean it, I'm going to have to pull over," came Emma's steel-edged voice.

"What's the big deal?" Sam asked, stretching. "It's just a little snow."

"Please, Sam, you don't understand," Emma said, gulping hard.

Sam finally focused on how weird Emma was acting. Her voice was shaking, her shoulders were hunched over, and her knuckles were white where her hands gripped the steering wheel.

"But, Em, you grew up in Boston and Switzerland, for Pete's sake! You must know how to drive in the snow!" Sam asked.

"Well, I don't!" wailed Emma. "I wasn't allowed to! Lawrence or one of the school's chauffeurs always drove me when it snowed!"

"You're kidding," Sam said.

"No, dammit, I'm not kidding!" Emma yelled. The car fishtailed again as Emma tried to slow down. Up ahead, cars were braking.

"Look," said Sam, leaning forward, "it's easy . . ."

They were fast approaching what looked like a traffic jam ahead.

Sam continued, trying not to alarm Emma, "Whatever you do, just don't slam on the—"

Emma slammed on the brakes.

Immediately the wheels locked and skidded on the slick road. The car went sliding toward the knot of cars ahead, making a soft crunching thud as the bumper of Emma's car hit the fender of the car in front of them.

Emma sat there for a second, dazed, then she and Sam got out of the car. The driver ahead, an older woman, met them by the fender. The woman wore snow boots and appeared to have on a warm-up suit topped by a plaid car coat and a red tam-o'-shanter spangled with large mirrored sequins. Both Emma and the woman began to assess the damage.

Emma's car looked like it would come away with only a scratch or two on the bumper. But the other woman's fender was deeply dented, mashed all the way up into the wheel well, though miraculously not pressing on the tire.

"My insurance will take care of this," Emma told her. "I'm just so sorry."

"Don't feel bad," said the woman, the pompom on top of her hat bobbing as she spoke. "I almost did the same thing to the car in front of me. Let's just hope the police get here before too long. Mitzi has an appointment at the beauty shop. I'm Camille Baker, by the way."

Sam and Emma introduced themselves. Sam, glancing in the back window of Camille's car, thought she was seeing things: a miniature tam, exactly like the one Camille was wearing, popped above the back seat, then vanished again.

"I suppose we can go ahead and trade insurance information," said Camille. "We can all sit in my car. There's plenty of room and Mitzi just loves to meet new people."

The mystery of the vanishing tam was solved when Camille opened the car door to a round of maniacal yapping. A bug-eyed chihuahua, wearing a matching red tam and sweater vest, greeted Camille with a series of canine acrobatics.

"This is Mitzi," said Camille. "Mitzi, say hello to the nice girls."

Mitzi greeted Emma with a bounding pirouette. But Sam, climbing into the back seat, found herself nose to nose with a snarling miniature Cujo.

"She doesn't like redheads," apologized Camille. "I don't know why. That and nail-biting are her only faults."

Sam and Mitzi maintained a standoff in the back seat while Camille scribbled down insurance information and rattled on about the fortune that could be made in bite-resistant doggie nail polish. It was a very long twenty minutes before a squad car got to them.

After accomplishing all the necessary paperwork, Emma found the policeman, an Officer Leeman, fixing her with a questioning gaze.

"Miss Cresswell," said Officer Leeman, "I called your license into our computer bank—purely routine, you understand. But I'm afraid you'll have to come with me to headquarters. Your friend can follow along in your car."

"Am I being cited for the accident?" Emma asked.

"No, ma'am," said the policeman. "We're putting that down to hazardous driving conditions."

Emma was cold and tired and she wanted to get to a hotel. "So what is the problem, then?"

"The problem," Officer Leeman said, "is that you are listed as a missing person."

Everyone was nice enough at police headquarters, but Emma had to put up with some chiding for not having gotten in touch with her father. Even Sam got into the act.

"It was stupid," Sam said bluntly. "It wouldn't have hurt to check in from Savannah. You knew then that he was looking for you. If you'd just done that, we wouldn't be sitting in this stupid police station right now."

That remark burned Emma. *If Sam doesn't understand about my family by now,* she thought, *there's no point in trying to explain.*

The real irony of the situation was that her father wasn't even reachable. According to Rosa, the housekeeper for the Palm Beach residence, he and Valerie had taken off for some island-hopping in the Caribbean. The fact that Emma left a message for him satisfied the highway patrol, who assured her that she'd be off the list of missing persons as soon as their computer network could circulate the information.

When they finally got out of the police station, the snow had deepened sufficiently to offer some traction. With Sam driving, they made good time. But Emma was wrapped in a dark cloud, angry at Sam for not understanding her, and angry at herself for being so wimpy. *Where is the new, carefree Emma?* she wondered.

I wish Carrie were here. Emma stared out the window morosely. *I need some mature advice, and Sam is not exactly the person to give it to me.*

Meanwhile, Sam was trying to pretend that Emma's freeze-out didn't hurt her feelings. *Honestly! Emma makes every little thing into World War Three! Sometimes she acts like the whole world revolves around her.* Sam, too, wished Carrie were there. Carrie always knew what to say to smooth out the rough spots between Emma and Sam. Besides, Sam was quite certain that Carrie would agree with her about how dumb Emma was acting.

Neither Emma nor Sam broke the silence, and they managed to hit the outskirts of New York City two hours later without having spoken one word to each other.

Once they reached Manhattan, however, Sam got too psyched to keep up the silent treatment, no matter how Emma felt. It was all just too exciting.

"Oh my God, I can't believe I'm in New York!" Sam exulted as they cruised south toward SoHo.

Even in the snowy weather the streets were teeming with action. People of every size, shape, and color were out on the streets. It was a constant parade of people.

Within moments of using her key to get into her Aunt Liz's SoHo loft, Emma had kicked off her shoes and headed into the kitchen, where she found a half-empty bottle of Chablis in the refrigerator.

"Want some?" she called to Sam as she poured herself a glass.

"No, thanks," Sam called back from the living room, where she was standing at the window looking down on the local scene. "I can't believe how hip this place is," Sam said in wonder.

Emma gulped down half a glass of wine and refilled her glass quickly. Aunt Liz's loft was looking better and better all the time.

Emma awoke the next morning with a pounding headache.

Hangover, she thought. Her stomach rolled over as she remembered last night's wine before dinner, wine with dinner, and the additional bottle she'd picked up on the way back to Aunt Liz's apartment.

Now she rummaged through her aunt's medicine cabinet for something she could use as a hangover remedy. Finally settling for aspirin-free pain reliever, she took two, then headed toward the kitchen to forage for something to settle her stomach.

"You look like dog meat," Sam said cheerfully from the kitchen table, where she sat sipping coffee.

"Actually, I feel fine," Emma said coolly. She wasn't about to admit her hangover to Sam, who had cautioned her several times the night before that she'd better eat more if she was going to keep drinking.

"Well, good," Sam said. "I'm glad you feel fine. So—I'm all ready to go when you are."

"I won't be more than fifteen minutes," Emma promised in her frostiest voice. She turned and headed for the shower.

I'm dying, a voice in her head told her as she held her head under the steaming hot water. *Why, why, why did I do this to myself?*

Fifteen minutes later Emma was ready to go. She wrote her aunt a thank-you note in a shaky hand, and left it propped up on the kitchen table.

Sam drove the first two hours out of New York, and Emma got some badly needed sleep. By the time she woke up her mood had improved greatly. *I'll never drink again,* she vowed to herself. She felt sane, sober, and ready to meet up with Carrie.

"There she is!" Sam yelled, opening the door and bolting from the car to hug Carrie as Emma eased into the space in front of Hummingbird, the café they'd decided on for lunch.

Emma was feeling better by then, but her energy still couldn't match Sam's, and for a moment she felt left out of things. Then Carrie was pulling Sam around to Emma's side of the car. Carrie opened the door, and she and Sam fairly dragged Emma out of the car and into a three-way embrace.

"Look at you!" cried Carrie, holding Emma at

141

arm's length, then stepping back. "Look at this car! I want to hear about every single adventure you two had—the uncut version!"

Emma thought she'd never been so glad to see Carrie. Dressed in jeans, a deep purple sweater that brought out the color of her velvet-brown eyes, and a wonderful scarf in muted tones of rose, blue, and purple, Carrie looked fresh, pretty, and confident. *Carrie can handle anything*, thought Emma. *Yale, a boyfriend or two, a career on the rise. I can't even handle my own family!* It occurred to Emma that Carrie might not even like her so much if she knew how weak she really was. The last time they'd been together, everything had seemed so clear. But now . . .

"You must be living right," Sam said, looking Carrie over as they were being seated for lunch. "You look as healthy as a horse!"

Carrie's face reddened, as if she'd been smacked.

"I know I look like a cow—" Carrie began.

"You don't!" Sam protested. "I didn't mean anything by that! You look great, that's all I wanted to say."

"Anything but the truth," Carrie murmured.

"That's ridiculous!" Sam cried. "You look fabulous!"

Sam meant what she said. To her, Carrie looked fabulous—poised, centered, totally together. And she certainly didn't look fat. *Now if only I could sneak some makeup onto that Ivory Girl face of hers, Carrie would be perfect.*

"I know I . . . gained a few pounds," Carrie said ruefully.

"Well, if you did, I certainly can't tell," Emma told her.

"You can't tell because I'm wearing baggy clothes again," Carrie pointed out honestly.

Even as she was saying this, a voice in Carrie's head was telling her to shut up. *Stop obsessing about your problems!* she instructed herself. She was determined to turn the conversation to something else. After all, no way could either Sam or Emma relate to the anguish of a weight problem.

"So how's the wonderful world of Disney?" Carrie asked Sam.

"Great!" Sam replied brightly, grabbing for a menu. "Let's eat, I'm starved!"

"I'm not very hungry," Emma murmured as she glanced at the wine list. Sam shot her an admonishing glance.

Don't start on me, Sam, thought Emma. *I'm going to relax and have a good time now that the three of us are together.* When the waiter appeared, she ordered a glass of claret, since no one else was interested in sharing a bottle.

Carrie was surprised to see Emma drinking wine at lunch, but then she remembered her friend's European education. People over there always drank wine with meals, and Emma certainly knew how to take care of herself.

"So tell me," Carrie asked when Emma's wine arrived and she and Sam were sipping on Diet Cokes, "how was life on the road?"

"Well, the truth of the matter," Sam began, "is that I've been breaking hearts all along the way."

"But I take it yours is still intact," Carrie said with a laugh.

"You take it correctly." Sam sighed and gave her friend a mournful look. "In more ways than one. But Boss-woman Cresswell here kept herding me along every time things started to look promising."

"You are so full of it, Sam!" Emma laughed. "I should have fed you to Tiger!"

"Tiger?" Carrie asked.

"I'd rather you'd have fed me to Ranger Ted!" Sam shot back with wide-eyed innocence.

"Ranger Ted?" Carrie echoed.

Sam and Emma started to argue playfully about their exploits on the road. "Gosh," said Carrie, "and I thought I was having fun with midterms!"

Finally the conversation turned to the future and Sunset Island, and Carrie filled her friends in on the fire at the Play Café and the benefit scheduled for their first night on the island.

"I might mention, Sam, that a certain Tennessee boy will be looking for you there," Carrie teased.

"Yeah, yeah," said Sam breezily. In fact, she was looking forward to seeing Pres again, though she was surprised at how often she'd thought of Danny this week. Not in fantasies, like the Ranger Ted thing. It was like she'd been sending

Danny mental postcards—she felt like he'd almost been along for the trip.

Carrie and Emma were both relieved when lunch ended without further mention of boyfriends. Carrie hadn't sorted out her feelings from that last terrible scene with Josh, and didn't want to talk about him or Billy either just yet. Emma knew that her friends would be watching to see what happened with Kurt, and found herself almost dreading it. He had hurt her so badly last summer, and right now she didn't feel very strong. What if she got to Sunset Island and Kurt didn't really want her back after all?

As they finished lunch and headed for the car, each of the girls was thinking ahead to the upcoming evening in Boston.

Thank God my mother won't be around, thought Emma. *I'll finally be able to have some real friends over. And I can get this stuff about Kurt off my chest. After all, these are my friends!*

Once we're at Emma's, it'll be just like old times, Sam thought. *We'll talk about real things. I'll come clean about getting fired. Emma and Carrie will understand, because they really, truly are my friends. And I'll talk to Emma about all that wine she's been drinking.*

Carrie, who'd run back in for a last stop in the bathroom to purge herself of her lunch, now hurried to the car where her friends waited.

She wasn't thinking about intimate conversations with her two best friends. She was thinking about how to keep her horrible secret from them, no matter what.

TEN

"Hey, look, Emma," said Carrie. "You've got lots of messages!"

The trio had just arrived at Emma's house, and amid the oohs and ahs of the tour, Carrie had discovered the calls indicator blinking rapidly on the answering machine. Her mother still maintained Emma's separate line and machine although Emma had pointed out to her several times that she was hardly ever there.

Kurt! thought Emma. She had called him from Aunt Liz's, but had gotten his answering machine. She'd left him a message that they'd be arriving on the four o'clock ferry on Saturday, and she'd hoped he might call to say he'd meet her. After hearing that Billy had called Carrie, and Pres had sent word (in a roundabout way) that he was looking for Sam, Emma needed to feel that someone was waiting eagerly for her, too.

She pressed the play button.

"Emma, where are you?" It was her mother's

voice. "The police have called here! Have you gotten yourself into some kind of trouble?"

The next message was also from her mother: "Emma, I had Lawrence call your apartment building today, and the building superintendent told him you've been gone for almost a week. I hope you're checking with at least one of your machines. Please call me immediately when you hear this!" She left a number where she was staying at Glen Echo.

"You didn't tell her about this trip?" Sam said to Emma incredulously.

"Of course I did! She didn't listen," Emma shot back.

"All right, Emma," went the next message, yet again from her mother, "I do seem to remember something about your leaving town. I'd still like to know how you ever got involved with the police. Call me." Was every one of these calls going to be from her mother?

Her mother again: "Emma, I finally reached your Aunt Liz, who said she just missed you in New York. Then the police called again to say you'd been found. Now that I know you're not lying dead somewhere, I'd like to know what this is all about."

Not for the first time in her life, Emma wished there were such a thing as a mind torpedo, something you could launch from your eyes to annihilate detestable objects. Right now her answering machine would be blown to smithereens.

Finally a male voice came over the speaker. It

only took a second for a feeling of disappointment to hit Emma's stomach. It wasn't Kurt.

"Hi Emma, hi Sam, hi Carrie, it's Danny. I'm in Boston, at Kevin's. You have the number, Sam. Give a call, okay?"

Carrie noticed that Emma looked glum as she reset the machine, but Sam's face had lit up in a happy grin.

"You haven't said much about Goofy," Carrie said to Sam. "What's the deal?"

"Danny's okay," Sam replied, a little surprised at how good his message had made her feel.

"He's also really considerate," Emma said with a sigh. Sam and Carrie knew what that sigh was about—Kurt hadn't called.

"Hey, Emma, is it okay if I use the phone?" Sam asked. "I want to call Danny."

"Maybe you ought to call your mom first, Emma," Carrie suggested.

"Might as well get it over with," Emma grumbled.

Carrie and Sam were kind enough to make themselves scarce, with the excuse of unpacking the car. In truth, they had already heard enough from Emma's mother for one day, and didn't want to hang around to watch Emma suffer through this call.

"Emma! Finally!" were Kat's first words.

"Mother, look, I'm sorry if I worried you—"

"Worried? Worried?" she screeched into the phone. "I've been frantic! Are you all right?"

"Really, I'm fine, Mother," Emma said in an

149

even voice. "I've been fine all along. I guess the police business was just a little misunderstanding I had with Dad."

"Well, I'm sure it was his fault, darling," Kat decided, without bothering to ask what the misunderstanding was. "You've heard the news, I suppose. About your father?"

"Um, I'm not sure . . ." Emma said carefully.

"He's trying to establish that I'm incompetent!" Kat spat her words into the telephone. "He's alleging that your inheritance is at stake, and claiming that he's acting on your behalf! I am absolutely livid!"

"Mother," Emma said, "I assure you he is not acting on my behalf."

"Thank you, sweetheart," Kat said, her voice softening. "I knew it couldn't be true. After all, you and I are best friends!"

Just then the headache began, as usual right at her temples. Her first thought was of a glass of wine—cool, fragrant, tart on the tongue . . . and the smooth feeling of softening around the edges that would accompany the taste . . .

". . . so of course I insisted that you'd be happy to testify!" Kat finished triumphantly.

Emma's attention snapped back to the phone conversation. "I'm sorry, Mother. What did you say?"

"I said I told my lawyer that your father was most certainly not acting on your behalf, and that you'd be happy to testify to that effect. I'm counting on you, Emma. My lawyer says your testimony could be essential."

"But Mother—"

"I'm thinking of getting you a device for recording your father's phone calls," Kat continued. "That way, we'll have concrete evidence if he tries anything."

Tears sprang to Emma's eyes, and she angrily wiped them away with the back of her hand. Was that all she was to her family? An inheritance for the lawyers to quibble over?

"Anyway, darling, we'll chat more about this later," Kat continued. "I'm really glad to know that you're fine."

"Sure, Mother," Emma said bitterly.

"Oh, my masseuse is just arriving," Kat said. "Must run! By the way, you had a call before I left from those Sunset Island people, the Hewitts? They're hoping you'll come back to work for them this summer, though I can't see why you'd want to do something like that again."

I'm sure you can't, thought Emma as she said a terse good-bye and hung up, thankful that the conversation with her mother was over.

By the time Sam and Carrie traipsed through the door with all their bags, Emma had a bottle of nice Beaujolais uncorked on the kitchen counter. She had thought to let it breathe for a little while, but had changed her mind and already poured herself a glass.

"Call Danny," Emma said to Sam, sipping her wine. "I just decided we're having a party."

"Hot damn!" Sam cried. "With food and guys and everything?"

"Everything!" Emma agreed.

"What time does it start?" Carrie asked as she carried a suitcase into a bedroom.

Emma took a long gulp of her wine. "How's right now sound?"

It was an hour and a half later when Sam, the first to be showered and dressed, leapt to answer Danny's knock at the door.

"Goofy!" Sam screamed, and cheerleader-jumped into Danny's arms. She covered his face with puppy-dog kisses.

"Down, girl, down!" Danny joked, but he clearly loved the way Sam was greeting him.

"It's sheer youthful exuberance," she assured him. "Don't take it personally."

Carrie had just entered the room and witnessed this greeting. "I have a feeling he wants to take it personally," she teased.

Whoops, better watch that stuff, Sam cautioned herself.

"So, come on in," she said with a broad gesture to include both Danny and the guy standing with him on the threshold.

"Sam, this is Kevin Logan," said Danny.

"Hi, Kevin," said Sam with a grin. She hoped that her smile made up for practically ignoring the guy when she'd first seen Danny. Kevin had a youngish, sweet-looking face, with dark eyes that danced with intelligence. He returned her smile with an easy charm.

"And I'm Carrie," Carrie said, introducing herself to Kevin. "Hey, Goof!" she added, giving Danny a hug.

"Please, I'm off duty," Danny said mock-seriously. "Don't call me that or my fans will mob me."

"Fortunately, we didn't invite any six-year-olds to this party," Sam laughed, "so you should be safe. I ordered lots of pizza, there's wine on the counter, beer and Cokes in the fridge. What's your poison?"

"A beer would be great," Kevin said, heading for the fridge.

Sam laughed. "I like a guy who makes himself at home."

"You want one, Danny?" Kevin asked with his head in the fridge.

"Sure," Danny agreed.

Kevin carried the beers into the living room and handed one to Danny. "This house is fantastic. Which one of you does it belong to?"

"Actually, it belongs to bachelorette number three, who has yet to make her appearance," Sam quipped.

"She's got interesting taste," Kevin said, quietly looking over the living room.

He reminds me of someone, Carrie thought. *Who is it?* Then she put her finger on it—her brother Matt! Kevin had the same intelligent, mischievous kind of eyes set in a baby face. Both were the sort of guy you felt comfortable with right away, maybe because they both seemed to be so comfortable with themselves.

Carrie and Kevin started a conversation, and Danny seemed to have eyes only for Sam. *She looks extra hot tonight*, Carrie noted. Sam was poured into her faded jeans, and braless under a black leotard top. She'd thrown an antique lace bed jacket over the leotard. On anyone else, the effect might be bizarre, but on Sam it looked sexy and perfect.

Carrie sighed and looked down at her own black stretch pants and oversized houndstooth blazer. Coverups. Carrie couldn't in a million years imagine being thin enough and confident enough to, first, go without a bra, and second, wear a bed jacket to a party.

"So Danny told me you're at Yale," Kevin said to Carrie as he sipped his beer. "Is it as tough as I think it is?"

Carrie gave a shrug and laughed. "I'd like to impress you and tell you how incredibly difficult it is, but let's face it, I have no basis for comparison!"

It turned out that Kevin was a journalism major at Boston University, and with Carrie's tremendous interest in photojournalism, they quickly got involved in an intense conversation.

Sam was equally involved in regaling Danny with her exploits on the road (well, perhaps she exaggerated a *little*), and before either girl realized it, a half-hour had passed.

Sam and Carrie exchanged a look. Where was Emma?

As if to answer their thoughts, Emma appeared just then wearing a simple white skirt and blouse that had been impeccably tailored by Ralph Lauren. With nothing more than mascara, lip gloss, and one-carat diamond studs in her earlobes, she managed to look stunningly perfect.

"Hello, hello, hello!" Emma cried gaily. Carrie thought her eyes looked a little glassy, and remembered that Emma had retired to her room earlier with a full glass of wine—her second.

Kevin and Danny were too mesmerized by her perfection to notice anything beyond it. Kevin eagerly introduced himself to the beautiful rich girl who lived in this house.

"Hi, Emma," said Kevin. "Great place you've got here."

"Actually, it's my mother's," Emma said.

Just then the pizza arrived. Emma already had the cash ready, and Carrie took charge, leaving Emma free to enjoy Kevin's company for a few minutes before they ate.

"Sorry to be late for my own party," Emma apologized. "My aunt called from New York. She's my favorite relative in the whole world." Why was she telling this to a perfect stranger? Was it the wine talking? *Oh, who cares*, Emma told herself. *For once, just stop thinking so much!*

"So why is she your favorite?" Kevin asked in a friendly voice.

"Well, the truth of the matter is," Emma began

in a confidential tone, "she's the only one in my family who even remotely cares about me."

"I'm sorry," Kevin said.

"Don't be!" Emma responded gaily. "Why should I care? I'm filthy rich! I'll simply *buy* a family to care about me!"

Although a bright smile was plastered on Emma's face, to her horror, she felt tears rising in her eyes.

"Hey, you two, chow time!" Sam called from the dining area.

"Oh, God, ignore me," Emma whispered. *This is so embarrassing! Crying in front of a total stranger!*

"Start without us!" Kevin called into the other room. He turned back to Emma. "You don't have to explain if you don't want to," he said gently.

"I'm such a cliché!" Emma laughed shakily. "The unloved little rich girl!"

"Hey, nobody ever said you're not allowed to be unhappy if you're rich," Kevin pointed out.

A tear slid all the way down Emma's cheek. "I had too much wine, that's all."

Kevin just sat there, waiting patiently. "Talk if you want, or don't if you don't want."

"I . . . I hate myself sometimes!" Emma blurted out. "It's so disgusting, so self-indulgent! When I think about people with real problems, poor people, sick people—"

"You're glad you're not one of them?" Kevin finished for her.

Emma had to laugh, even if his humor was a

little dark. "Yes, I'm glad I'm not one of them," she admitted. "But I feel like I don't have any right to complain about anything. . . ."

While everyone else started in on the pizza, Kevin stayed in the kitchen with Emma. Slowly, he asked easy questions about the trip north, drawing Emma out of her weepy spell. Before long, he had her laughing as she described her dance with Sonny. She was grateful he hadn't probed too deeply about the causes of her sadness. It was bad enough that she had already blurted out that her family didn't love her. Talking with Kevin made her feel so . . . normal.

By the time they rejoined the others, sides were being chosen for a game of Pictionary. Kevin got Emma a Coke, and threw a few pieces of pizza in the microwave for them to eat as they played.

"Guess what?" Sam said with excitement. "Danny's coming with us to Sunset Island!"

"Sam!" Danny objected. "You were supposed to *ask* her, not *tell* her!"

"Hey, Carrie said it's fine," Sam countered. "Majority rules."

"It's Emma's car," Danny pointed out. He was really embarrassed.

"It's fine, Danny," Emma said warmly. "Did your ski plans fall through?"

Sam guffawed. "No, he fell through . . . he fell right through his costume!"

"I sprained my back," said Danny sheepishly.

"You guys gotta hear this story!" Sam yelled with glee.

"Go ahead, Sam, tell it," Danny sighed. "As if I could stop you."

"Okay, you know those baby strollers some people have, the ones the size of a small Mercedes? Well, one day Danny—a.k.a. Goofy—is plying his trade, and some woman was letting her oldest kid push the baby. The kid runs the stroller right up alongside Goofy's leg, hooking the costume on one of the wheel bolts. The kid starts yelling 'Leggo! Leggo!' at Danny, but he keeps right on pushing!"

"The head of that costume is gigunda," Danny added. "I couldn't even see the kids or the stroller till I tripped. Luckily I didn't smash them on my way down."

"Poor Danny!" Emma exclaimed. "Sounds like an off-season week on Sunset Island is just what you need." She turned to Kevin. "So you're left without a ski partner?"

"I'll handle it," Kevin replied. "It's just for the weekend. My cash flow can't hack more than that, anyway."

"Hey, why don't you come up, too?" Carrie asked Kevin spontaneously. "We're giving a big party next Saturday."

"That's a great idea!" Danny agreed. "Sam says there's a motel that should be mega-cheap in the off season."

"Are you sure it's okay?" Kevin asked.

"It'd be a total blast!" Sam assured him.

They agreed that Danny would ride with them the next day, and Kevin would meet them on the island on Monday. When they finished the Pictionary game, the guys got ready to leave. Kevin wanted to start for the slopes before dawn. He gave Emma a special hug before he left. That brief moment managed to convey a lot of caring and concern. Emma was touched.

Sam walked out with them, and Carrie and Emma noticed Danny taking her hand as they left.

"You think Sam would even know it if she was in love?" Carrie asked Emma as they watched them go.

"I'm probably the last person on earth anyone should ask about love right now," Emma said sadly. "Kurt didn't even call me."

From the window they watched Kevin and Danny getting into Kevin's car. "I'll tell you something, Carrie," Emma said in a soft voice. "Kevin Logan is a truly decent guy, one of the nicest guys I've ever met. If it doesn't work out with Kurt, I hope he's still around."

"I know just what you mean," said Carrie. "Whoever gets him will really have a prize."

Sam bounded back through the door, looking pleased with herself. "Fellow vixens, I ask you—can I pick them or can I pick them? Two—count 'em, two—gorgeous guys have just been added to our island repertoire."

"You know, I think Danny's crazy about you, Sam. I wouldn't treat that lightly if I were you."

"Ah, well," said Sam breezily, "so many men, so little time. Now where's the rest of that pizza? I forgot to pig out!"

Carrie got up and excused herself quickly from the room.

Emma was feeling so much better, she decided to have a last glass of wine before bedtime. Maybe she'd get up the nerve to share some of her anxieties about Kurt with Sam and Carrie.

Sam decided to redo her nails, now that it was back to all-girl company. Fishing through her makeup bag in Emma's guest room, she was thinking that now might be a good time to tell her friends about her unemployed status. All of a sudden she noticed sounds coming from behind the adjoining bathroom door.

"Carrie?" she called, then knocked. "Are you okay?"

There was almost a minute of silence, and Sam was about to knock again. Then the door opened, and Carrie walked right into the room as if nothing were wrong.

"Hey!" said Sam, taking her by the shoulders. "Are you okay?"

"I'm fine," said Carrie.

"Fine, hell! I heard you being sick in there. Why didn't you tell anybody you weren't feeling good? Was it the pizza?"

"I think it's just me. You know, I'm kind of overwrought," Carrie lied. "I didn't want to spoil the evening."

"Well, for God's sake, get right into bed and get

some rest!" Sam blustered. "It could be a bug, and we can't have you spreading germs around!"

Cowed by Sam's good intentions, and ashamed of herself, Carrie let herself be fussed over and tucked into bed. Sam moved to the living room to do her nails while Emma sipped her wine. But the promise had gone out of the evening.

And they didn't really feel much like talking after all.

ELEVEN

Saturday dawned crisp and cloudless, with the sun glinting off the melting remains of the snow. Sam, Carrie, and Emma picked up Danny on a corner near Boston University, and decided to put Boston behind them before stopping for breakfast.

"Can I drive?" Carrie asked as Danny got into the back of the car.

"Sure," Emma told her, and acted as if she was doing something nice for Carrie. The truth of the matter was that she still had the dull headache she'd woken up with—a headache she'd come to recognize as being caused by drinking too much wine before bed.

They stopped for breakfast at a place advertising family dining.

"Make that two western omelettes," Sam told the waitress after Danny had ordered one ahead of her. "No, make that four western omelettes." She stared at Carrie and Emma. "You two look like you need a protein infusion!"

163

"I can order my own food," Emma said tersely.

"Well, excuse me for caring," Sam said.

Emma rubbed her temples. "I'm sorry. I woke up on the wrong side of the bed."

Breakfast put everyone into a better mood. The orange juice seemed to revive Emma and she soon felt almost human.

By the time Danny took the wheel after breakfast, they were singing old camp songs together.

"*B-I-N-G-O*, and Bingo was his name-o!" they all sang together, cracking up.

"Now how is it that these same stupid songs made their way from Camp Winnemucca in Kansas all the way to some snooty camp in the Berkshires?" Sam asked, since Emma knew the words to the camp songs as well as anybody else.

"It reaches even farther than that!" Emma laughed. "I learned that song at a summer retreat outside of Paris for daughters of the hideously rich."

"Wow! International nonsense songs!" Carrie marveled.

"I've got to teach that one to Katie this summer," Emma said with a soft smile on her face.

Sam looked surprised. "I take it that means you've decided to work for the Hewitts again."

Emma shrugged and wound a strand of hair around her finger. "My mother told me they called and asked me to."

"I'm not surprised they asked," Carrie said. "You were great with their kids last summer."

Emma gave Carrie a smile of gratitude.

"I don't know, I haven't committed yet," Emma said. "I guess I thought I'd have a . . . new direction or something by this summer. How about you two?" she asked her friends.

"I've been thinking about it, too," Carrie admitted. "Listen, we could all do worse than another summer on Sunset Island. Graham and Claudia told me at Christmas they were hoping to hire me again, but they didn't know yet where they'd be. If there's a European tour or something, I'll be out of a job."

Emma turned around to face Sam in the back seat. "How about you? Sunset Island would never be the same without you."

"What makes you think Dan Jacobs won't need my help again?" asked Sam a little indignantly. "With those twin monsters of his, he'd be lucky if anyone else would want the job!"

"I'm sure he'll want you back, Sam," said Carrie, "but would you really quit your job at Disney World just to be an au pair for the summer?"

The car swerved slightly as Danny whipped around to give Sam a funny look.

"What?" Emma asked, noting the look.

"Nothing," Danny mumbled, but the expression on his face belied his words.

A day of following highways up the coast of Maine brought them to the ferry dock with plenty of daylight left.

Emma was glad to see that hers was one of the

only cars in line for the auto ramp—the ferry couldn't hold more than a few. After a brief walk to stretch her legs, she returned to the car, letting the others wander on their own. The sun was still warm, and now that the car was stopped, she decided to put the top down.

Seating herself on top of the back seat, Emma gazed at the water and let her thoughts flow ahead to the island and Kurt. Kurt. She warned herself not to get her hopes up, even though just the thought of him made her heart pound in her chest. *I mean, he didn't even care enough to call me in Boston.* And yet she couldn't seem to shake this feeling of hopefulness. Wasn't it possible that they really had a chance? That this summer they both would have matured enough to have the kind of relationship that Emma longed for?

Carrie, too, was wandering around the dock, lost in thought. As soon as they had arrived at the ferry station she'd headed for the ladies' room. Her weight-loss plan was way off schedule. Somehow she wasn't purging often enough—it seemed as if Sam or Emma was always around, ready to catch her. It had been bad enough trying to talk Sam out of her firm conviction that Carrie had had a stomach virus the other night.

Carrie shut her eyes and leaned against the wall of the ferry station. God, it was so horrible, lying to her friends and hiding shamefully in a toilet, throwing her guts up. And maybe the most horrible part of the whole thing was that her friends would never, ever in a million years believe that she, Carrie Alden, supergirl, was capable of such sick, disgusting behavior.

While Carrie and Emma were lost in their private thoughts, Sam and Danny were having a difficult conversation at the end of the dock.

"I feel like a fifth wheel, if you really want to know!" said Danny.

"How can you be a fifth wheel? There are only four of us here," Sam said innocently.

"That's not what I'm talking about, and you know it," Danny said angrily. "We come all this way and you just casually mention to me that you've got a guy waiting for you on the island. What did you expect me to say?"

"Well, see, the thing is that he may be waiting for me, but that doesn't mean I'm waiting for him," Sam explained.

Danny looked disgusted. "What are you talking about?"

Sam bit her lower lip. This was not going at all the way she had planned. She had thought that making Danny jealous would do wonderful things for her love life. Visions of Pres and Danny fighting over her had filled her head. Only now it seemed that Danny was really, truly angry. She hadn't counted on that.

"What I mean," Sam said slowly, "is that he's just a guy I went out with. It's not like he's my boyfriend."

"Went out with?" Danny repeated. "And just what is that supposed to mean?"

"You know," Sam floundered. "Like you and I go out. Not heavy."

"So you and this Pres guy don't have a romantic relationship, is that it?"

"Uh, well . . ." This was getting tougher and tougher. In truth, her relationship with Pres was strictly romantic—all excitement and not much substance. She had a feeling Danny wouldn't take much comfort in that.

"If you mean am I sleeping with him, the answer's no," she finally managed, trying her best to look confident and cool.

Danny gave her a level gaze and folded his arms. "I think my question is more like, do you want to sleep with him?"

Ooh, tough question. One part of her desperately wanted to sleep with Pres. Another part of her wanted to run in the other direction as fast as she could.

"Sam, I asked you a question," Danny repeated. "Do you want to sleep with him?"

"I don't know," Sam answered truthfully.

Because it was the most honest answer she'd given anyone in a long time, she was totally unprepared for Danny's reaction.

"And why should I believe that?" he exploded. "You'll lie to anyone about anything if it suits your purposes!"

"Danny, I—"

"It's true!" Danny shot back at her. "You're still lying to your best friends about losing your job!"

168

With a final gesture of disgust, Danny turned on his heel and walked briskly away from Sam.

In the back seat of the car, Emma jumped to her feet. The ferry was coming! Craning to get a better look, she could just make out the silhouettes of those passengers riding on the deck. The boat drew closer and her heart leapt. Was she seeing what she thought she was seeing? She blinked rapidly, but the sight on the deck of the ferry still riveted her. Kurt. Kurt was on the ferry. As her heart soared he lifted his arm and waved in her direction.

"Oh Emma, how romantic!" Carrie cried, coming up next to Emma. "He came over to meet you!"

"I can't believe it!" was all Emma could think to say.

"Well, what are you waiting for?" Carrie said with a laugh. "This is just like a movie—go throw yourself into his arms!"

Emma didn't know exactly how she traveled the short distance from the car to the dock, but suddenly she was there, and there was Kurt, and the next thing she knew she was in his arms.

"You came to meet me," she whispered, her eyes shining up into his.

As for Kurt, he seemed at a loss for words. He just kept repeating her name softly, over and over.

Somehow Emma managed to introduce Danny and get her car squared away for the ride, but all these details went by in a haze. She was with

Kurt again, and that was the only thing that mattered right now.

Carrie passed the ferry ride thinking only of Billy. Her troubles with Josh seemed far away now, and she was glad she hadn't had the chance to tell Emma and Sam about their quarrels.

On board, Sam was relieved to find Danny beside her.

"You still speaking to me?" she asked him with a sidelong look.

"So it appears," he answered, but he didn't quite make eye contact with her as he said it.

"So, do you hate me, loathe me, never want to speak to me again, or what?" Sam asked him.

"All of the above," he said, but this time there was a definite laugh in his voice.

"Okay, so I drive you nuts," Sam allowed, happy to see a smile starting to break out on Danny's face.

"You do," Danny agreed. "And listen," he said, turning serious again for a moment, "you can play this silly game with me if you want to. For the moment, anyway. But I really do think that lying to Emma and Carrie is beat."

"When you're right, you're right," Sam said lightly. "But I have to handle it my own way. Now, how about if we just go have some fun?"

Once the ferry got away from the boat basin and picked up speed, Danny stood behind Sam on the deck, and Sam leaned against him, the wind lifting her hair back from her face. Kurt and Emma were so lost in each other that they might as well have been sitting on a cloud. And Carrie was completely absorbed in thoughts of Billy. The wind was a little sharp on the water, but they all staunchly stayed on deck.

And then, finally, there it was on the horizon—Sunset Island. Each girl thought about how different she had felt traveling on that same ferry when she'd come to begin her job the summer before. Then, it had been a strange place, even a bit frightening. But now each of them smiled eagerly at the approaching shoreline—they couldn't wait to get there. In a way, it was home.

They left the top of Emma's car down for the drive to the Play Café, where the Flirts were setting up for the benefit that night. Emma drove, with Kurt sitting up front and Carrie, Sam, and Danny wedged in the back. Everyone talked and laughed at once, pointing out landmarks to one another and playing tour guide for Danny.

"The Cheap Boutique! I love that store," Sam cried ecstatically when they reached the shops located on what was known as the rock-and-roll side of the island.

"Wow, look at the side of the Play Café," Emma said as she parked the car. "You can see the fire damage."

"I'm just so happy to see it at all!" Sam yelled. "God, I love this place!"

Kurt got out of the passenger seat and, like a flash, Carrie followed. Billy came out of the café and she ran into his arms.

"Do you know how good you feel?" he whispered to her huskily.

"No, tell me," she said with a grin.

"Do you think anyone would notice if I threw you on the ground and ravished you right here and now?" Billy asked, wrapping his arms even more tightly around Carrie.

"I'd notice," Carrie said solemnly, "but I'd like it!"

Billy pulled back to give her a wickedly promising smile, then turned to the group who had just made their way to the front door.

"Come on in. You're just in time for one of our world-famous sunsets." Taking Carrie's arm, he led the way.

Inside, the stage area was a tangle of cables and equipment, with people moving here and there amid the clutter. An odor of smoke was still barely detectable, reminding everyone of the purpose of all this mayhem.

Sam didn't see Pres at first. She could feel Danny's eyes watching her. He knew Pres was in Billy's band. And then, there he was, standing up from behind an amplifier he'd been connecting.

Sam's eyes met Presley's, and her heart did a flipflop.

The guy was a serious, total, maximum, studly fox. Had he gotten even better-looking since she'd last seen him, or had her memory failed her?

Pres stepped down from the stage as Sam

started across the floor, leaving Danny, stranded and ill at ease, to watch.

"Well, look what just blew into town," Pres drawled, his eyes taking in all of Sam. "You are one fine sight, girl."

"Mutual," Sam acknowledged.

"You been keepin' busy?"

"I'm a professional dancer now," Sam told Pres proudly.

"Watching you move was always a thing of beauty," Pres said with a grin.

Sam looked quickly behind her at Danny's stricken face. Yikes. This was horrible. She had thought she'd feel like an incredibly sexy, desirable woman if she flirted with both guys. But now that the three of them were actually in the same room, all she felt was anxious and embarrassed.

"Hey, come on down and meet my friend," Sam told Pres.

Pres gave Sam a big kiss hello and then ambled across the room with her until they stood in front of Danny.

"Danny, this is Presley Travis, bass player for the infamous band, Flirting with Danger. Pres, meet Danny Franklin, my best friend from Orlando."

Sam breathed a silent sigh of relief as Danny and Pres shook hands. So far so good. There hadn't been any actual bloodshed.

"First time on Sunset Island?" Pres asked Danny.

"Yeah," answered Danny in his typical mono-syllabic fashion.

"Don't worry, we'll show you a good time," promised Pres. He turned to Sam. "I'll see you later—that's a promise," he murmured, then went back to setting up.

"See?" Sam tried to comfort Danny with a grin and a little tug on his sleeve. "We're all friends here."

"Yeah," said Danny, not looking too sure.

"Oh no," Carrie groaned, her face turned toward the front door. "Look what the cat just dragged in."

Emma and Sam turned around to see Lorell Courtland and Diana De Witt sashaying their way into the Play Café.

"I feel a headache coming on, and it's walking right toward me," Emma managed.

Lorell Courtland and Diana De Witt were the last two people in the world that the girls wanted to see. As far as Emma, Sam, and Carrie were concerned, Diana and Lorell were two of the most obnoxious, evil, manipulative, bitchy humans on the face of the earth. Lorell had alleg-edly worked on the island last summer as an au pair for the Pope family, but the truth was that she had just used their house to change her clothes. Both she and Diana were filthy rich, and they made sure everyone knew it. Emma had gone to school with Diana. They had been arch-enemies for fourteen years. And it was Diana with whom Kurt had had his fling last summer, breaking Emma's heart.

"If you ask me," Sam offered tartly, "someone left the gate open at the dog pound, and two of the bitches escaped."

Emma licked her lips nervously and looked at Kurt. It had never occurred to her that she might have to face Diana in a showdown so soon.

"Everything's fine, Emma," Kurt whispered, holding Emma even closer. "She can't hurt us now."

"Well, well, what have we here?" Lorell purred to Diana in that sickening Southern accent of hers. "As I live and breathe, it's my favorite trio!"

"Hello, Kurt," crooned Diana, her eyebrows raised smugly. She reached out one manicured hand and clasped his bicep. Only then did she deign to notice Emma.

"Why, Emma!" Diana said, wide-eyed. "What a surprise to see you here!"

"Hello, Diana, hello, Lorell," Emma said coolly. "My, my, Lorell, the last time I saw you it was Christmas, and you were throwing yourself at Flash Hathaway on a yacht. That was one of the more amusing moments of my life, I must admit."

Diana turned to look at Lorell. "You went out with Flash Hathaway?" she asked with surprise.

Flash Hathaway was a cretinous photographer known for offering his photographic services and then trying to get into a girl's pants. Sam had had a run-in with him the summer before.

"No, no, I just went to a Christmas party with him on a yacht," Lorell explained hastily.

"That's not what you told us at the time," Sam reminded her, enjoying every word. "You told us it was true love." Sam made loud smooching noises in Lorell's direction.

"Lorell?" Diana asked, wrinkling her nose in disgust.

"Oh, puh-leeze!" Lorell shot back. "Are you goin' to take the word of these lowlifes? I might have dated him once or twice. He's crazy for me, if you want to know."

"I don't," Carrie whispered under her breath.

"But anyway, at this point in my life I'm lookin' for a more mature, more open kind of a relationship," Lorell explained, her eyes running over Danny as she spoke.

"Really?" Sam commented, feigning interest.

"You know what that means, don't you?" Lorell asked, staring right at Danny.

"Gee, I get confused, Lorell," Sam said, screwing up her face. "Does it mean open to ridicule, or just to transmittable diseases?"

"Well, I guess a girl like you, who needs to get tested regular for such things, would know," Diana said, brushing her curls out of her face.

"What are you two doing here, anyway?" Kurt asked the poisonous twosome.

Diana looked hurt. "Why, Kurt, you called and invited me!"

The sharp intake of Emma's breath could have

been heard clear out by her car. She turned to look at Kurt.

"You are full of it, Diana," Kurt said, his voice full of steel. "You know that isn't true."

"But Emma didn't," Diana said with a smug grin on her face. Diana raised her chin and stared Emma down. "Better be careful, Emma. I can see that you're none too confident about lover boy here. I got him once, and I can get him again."

"Did anyone ever mention how completely disgusting you are?" Sam asked Diana, stepping closer to her. Sam's hands were curled into fists. If Diana or Lorell said one more horrible thing, she was going to deck one of them.

"Come on, Diana," Lorell said, tugging on her friend's arm. "Let's come back later, when the music starts. The company in here is just too tacky for words."

"Totally without class," Diana agreed, heading for the door.

"Better than being without a clue!" Sam called after them.

Carrie smoothed the last hair into place and observed herself in the mirror with momentary satisfaction.

They'd barely had time for dinner after dropping Danny at the Bay View Motel and checking into their suite at the Sunset Inn. Carrie had straggled behind after dinner, and had ducked into the hotel lobby's rest room to get rid of her dinner, which had made her late in getting ready to leave.

Fixing her hair hardly mattered though, she told herself as she stared at her reflection. It wasn't like she spent any time putting on makeup or was doing anything special with her looks. Why was it that just because she'd gained weight it made her not want to take any care with her appearance? she wondered. Although her friends seemed to think she looked fine. At the last minute she'd thrown her new raspberry-colored blazer over her black stretch pants and black T-shirt. Did it really look okay? She'd lost all sense of perspective.

Carrie pushed through the door just as the band was striking up their opening number, "With You Again," a song Billy had sent her on tape with a note saying he'd written it for her. Could he really care about her if she was over-weight? And was it really possible he hadn't even noticed? He certainly hadn't said anything to her about it.

"Hey, I guess this is the last we'll see of you for a day or so," Emma teased, gliding up behind her and giving her a little nudge. It was understood that the fold-out sofa in the suite would probably stay folded up, as Carrie would most likely spend her nights with Billy.

"Well, we'll see," Carrie demurred. Suddenly she thought she'd feel embarrassed being alone with Billy. She'd feel fat.

"That was not spoken like a lovesick fool,"

Emma said, feeling Carrie's forehead as though testing to see if she was sick.

I'm acting nuts, Carrie told herself. After all, Billy had been up at school visiting her since she'd gained weight. It had never seemed to bother him. Or was he just being nice?

"Hey, what great thoughts are you thinking?" Emma asked Carrie lightly.

"I . . . I was thinking that actually you and Kurt probably wish you could be alone together. Maybe Sam will make a choice between Danny and Pres, or something."

"Actually, I don't want to be alone with Kurt," Emma whispered confidentially.

Carrie looked shocked. "Excuse me?"

"I mean, I do, of course I do," Emma added hastily. "But after everything that happened between us last summer, I'm in go-slow mode. I want to be sure this time."

Just then Kurt arrived with a glass of wine for Emma and a beer each for Carrie and himself. Conversation halted while they watched and listened to the band. The room was packed to capacity, but Sam stood out in a shocking pink tiger-striped bodysuit under a man's old fashioned black vest. Standing next to her was Danny, looking morose. Sam's eyes were glued to the sexy image of Pres playing bass up on the stage.

Carrie felt really bad for Danny. She knew he was crazy about Sam—it was totally obvious. But Sam had him coming and going.

"Look at Danny standing over there," Carrie yelled to Emma over the music. "He's such a sweetheart. I could throttle Sam."

"Oh, you know Sam," Emma began. "She—"

"Uh, excuse me," came a soft voice next to Emma.

Emma practically did a double take. "Daphne?"

Standing next to Emma was Daphne Whittinger, best friend of Lorell Courtland and Diana De Witt. The last time Emma had seen Daphne, in this very club, Daphne had tried to slice her face with a shard of glass. Only Kurt's timely intervention had prevented it. Daphne had been taken away to the hospital to treat her severe anorexia nervosa and probable addiction to diet pills. That was the last anyone had seen or heard from her.

"Emma, don't walk away," Daphne said quickly before Emma could respond. "I . . . I have something I've needed to say to you ever since last summer."

"I'm listening," Emma said. She noticed that Daphne had definitely gained weight since the previous summer. She looked clear-eyed, lucid, almost normal.

"You were right last summer when you told me I was sick, Emma," Daphne hurried on. "I ended up in the hospital for a long time. I found out I have what's called an eating disorder."

Emma nodded. That was all the encouragement Daphne needed to continue.

"I've . . . I've been in this recovery program

180

since then," she continued earnestly. "I'm getting better. I mean, I'm learning to forgive myself. Maybe someday you can forgive me, too," she finished.

"Listen, Daphne, you weren't responsible," Emma began. But before she could get any further Daphne had melted into the crowd and was gone.

"Did that really happen just now?" Emma asked Carrie. "*Quel* bizarre!"

But before any of them could utter a word, Carrie heard her name being called from another direction. She turned to find Claudia Templeton opening her arms for an embrace.

"I've been looking all over for you!" exclaimed Claudia. "Graham and I just popped in for the first set. We're leaving for Bangor, then on to Toronto in the morning, then to Scandinavia for two weeks!"

Carrie felt off balance—so much was happening at once! She stood back and let Claudia carry the conversation.

Graham had been offered a tour of Scandinavia, with enough time between concerts so that he and Claudia could have a kind of second honeymoon. When they'd heard about the benefit at the café, they'd wanted to contribute. Not only were they giving a generous donation, but Graham was going to make a guest appearance to close out the Flirts' set.

"So all this means that he'll be cutting the next album over the summer, and we'll be here on the island," Claudia said, wrapping up. "We've been desperate to find out if you'll be coming back, too."

Suddenly Carrie knew that that was what she wanted more than anything. The chance to be on Sunset Island again, to slow down and figure out what the hell was going on with her life.

"I'd love to!" she told Claudia happily, adding a hug to clinch the deal.

"The kids will be thrilled," said Claudia, "and so will Graham. We'll always be grateful for what you did for him last Christmas."

Carrie's efforts the previous winter had helped Graham face his second bout with a cocaine addiction, a battle he now appeared to be winning— with luck, for good this time.

Emma and Kurt had disappeared, and Carrie and Claudia kept up their visit between songs. By the time Claudia left to wait by the stage for Graham—they'd have to race to make the last ferry—Carrie had been invited to stay at the Templetons' house while she was on the island. They had already given the okay for the girls to have their party there. In fact, it had been Claudia and Graham's idea as soon as they heard about Carrie's spring break plans.

"Invite everyone and have all the fun you want. Just leave the place like you found it. We trust you, Carrie," Claudia had said.

Now Carrie watched with a warm glow as Graham took the stage. How lucky she was to have the trust and affection of such a loving family—and the family of a famous rock star to boot!

After rapturous applause, the audience settled in, mesmerized by Graham's performance of "Roll On," his latest hit. As the song moved into the second verse, Carrie was jostling through the swaying bodies for a better view when Sam came bursting through the crowd.

"Carrie!" Sam cried, a wild look in her eyes. "Have you seen Danny? I can't find him anywhere!"

He probably felt ignored and left, thought Carrie, but to Sam she simply said, "No, I haven't."

Sam went careening on in her search, and by the time Carrie reached the front, the song was ending. Graham saw her, though, and threw her a kiss and a wink before he and Claudia bolted out the door. She knew Billy would unwind with the guys for a few minutes before coming to find her. She propped her back against the stage to wait.

"Are you Carrie?" asked a slender, exotic-looking girl, walking up to Carrie with an outstretched hand. She looked to be in her early twenties—older, hip, very confident.

"Yes," said Carrie, surprised. She didn't remember ever seeing this girl before.

"I'm Luann," said the girl, clasping Carrie's hand for a quick, firm shake. "I've heard so much about you from Billy."

"Oh," said Carrie with what she hoped passed for a smile. She couldn't help it—her radar went up. *Who's this girl to Billy, anyway?* "I hope he said something good," Carrie added.

"Maybe too good," Luann said with a rueful laugh. "You probably have a better chance than I do."

Icy fingers of dread wound their way around Carrie's heart.

"Well," continued Luann, "I'm not the jealous kind, so I figured I'd come right out and introduce myself. I hate gossip."

Carrie was trying to fathom this when she looked up to see Billy staring wide-eyed at her and Luann from backstage. He ducked away quickly, trying to pretend he hadn't noticed them.

Luann had seen him, too, and now gave Carrie a knowing smile.

"After all, we might as well get to know each other," she said with a meaningful look in Billy's direction. "We do have a lot in common."

Carrie's mind was whirling as Luann strode purposefully toward the bar. In the past forty-five minutes, she had been bombarded with so much new information, she hardly knew how to sort it out. Her emotions were going in ten different directions.

Not even the hideous truth that she and Daphne Whittinger had something in common seemed to stay in her consciousness. She was too busy letting the truth register: Billy had another girl-friend.

TWELVE

"I figured this was where you had to be," said Billy, standing on the front steps of the Templetons' house. "Did you have to take off without a word last night?"

It was nine o'clock Sunday morning, and though Carrie was up and dressed, she felt exhausted.

"Come on in," she said quietly.

She led him into the Templetons' spacious living room and through to the sunny kitchen. She had felt safe there the moment she'd found the key in its hiding place last night. Now she was grateful to be on familiar ground.

"Did it ever occur to you that people would worry about you?" Billy asked. "I couldn't find Sam or Emma after you just walked out last night. This morning I finally thought of checking here."

"I left word at the inn where I'd be," Carrie said in a low voice.

Billy turned her to face him, gripping her shoulders hard. "Come on, Carrie."

Carrie took a step away from him. "Is this pretend-Carrie-is-special time?"

Billy looked stunned. "How can you say that?"

"Look, Billy, I'm not stupid, and I hate stupid games. I know you saw your friend Luann talking to me last night. She told me she's going out with you. Imagine my having to find that out from her."

"Hey—" Billy began.

"I was going to talk to you about it. I figured it was the only mature thing to do," Carrie said with an ironic twist to her mouth, "but when I found you backstage a little while later, Luann had found you first. Maybe you didn't see me because your face was buried in her hair."

Billy sighed and took a couple of paces away. He gazed out the sliding glass doors to the deck. He didn't speak for a moment.

"I only met her a few weeks ago," he finally said. "And I told her all about you."

"So she said," Carrie retorted. "Funny that you didn't bother to tell me all about her."

"I was going to, I really was," implored Billy. "Do you think I'd have wanted you to come up here if there was anyone else I was serious about?"

"As far as I knew," Carrie shot back, "there wasn't anyone else at all."

Billy's mouth drew into a thin line. "Listen, Carrie, I've known all along there was someone else in your life—you see him every day!"

"Hey, that's different—" Carrie began.

186

"Different how?" Billy shot back. "You expect me to sit up here like a damn mummy in a tomb, only coming to life when you arrive to dig me up?"

"But . . . but that just isn't fair!" Carrie sputtered. "Josh is my friend! He's been my best friend for years! It's nothing like you and me!"

"God, Carrie, wake up!" Billy said. "Do you really think you can have a long-term romantic relationship with Josh and then *poof!*—one day he's just your good buddy?"

"No, but—"

"I've seen how Josh looks at you. I know how he feels about you," Billy said. "You think I like it when we run into him at Yale?"

"How dare you twist this around?" Carrie cried. She put one hand on her forehead. How could this be happening? When she'd taken that long, cold walk to the Templetons' house last night, she'd been so full of righteous anger. But now Billy was putting her on the defensive!

Billy stared out the window again, as if trying to control his temper. Carrie hadn't even known he *had* a temper—she'd never seen it before.

"What I'm saying," Carrie began shakily, "is that it was rotten of you not to have told me about Luann before I got here. Can we just stick to that subject for the moment?"

Billy looked down guiltily. "It just didn't seem important enough."

"Billy, that is bull," Carrie said, folding her arms.

"Okay, maybe I felt a little bummed about it," Billy allowed.

"Well, at least you're being honest," Carrie said quietly.

Billy walked to Carrie and took hold of her shoulders. "Carrie, she is not important to me, that really is the truth," Billy whispered, staring into her eyes. "I like her very much, but she's not—you."

"Really?" Carrie asked. She needed his reassurance so badly.

"Really," he said firmly. He leaned in and kissed her softly on the lips. "How about if we go have breakfast, maybe take a walk on the beach, and talk about this?"

"You're on," Carrie said. "I'll get my jacket."

As Carrie went for her jacket she thought that maybe, just maybe, the situation with Billy wasn't as dire as her fears had led her to believe. But as she caught a look at her reflection in the hall mirror, her heart sank. Luann was so lovely and slender. How could Billy possibly prefer her over Luann?

By Monday morning, Sam was ticked. It was the second day in a row she'd found herself waking up alone in the suite at the Sunset Inn. Something was up, and no one was telling her anything.

Emma hadn't yet spent a night in her bed, and Sam suspected she and Kurt must be sleeping together. She was a little hurt that Emma hadn't confided in her. And Carrie, of course, had moved to the Templetons' house for the week. Sam could see why she'd prefer that over the bachelor pad the Flirts shared. But it was funny— Billy didn't seem to be staying there with her.

They had all been together the day before for a spontaneous Sunday-afternoon fun-and-games party at the Flirts' house.

Fun and games, my ass! thought Sam, remembering the stilted atmosphere of the gathering. They'd played a few games, but no one had seemed to be having much fun. Sam had noted that Emma, who had sipped wine all afternoon, had been pie-eyed and wobbly on her feet by the time Kurt whisked her out the door. But by then, Sam had had her own worries to contend with.

Damn that Danny! Sam seethed. Danny's absence the day before had been conspicuous. Sam had made a big show of flirting with Pres, but inside, she was bummed out. Emma and Carrie had seemed a little reproachful when they'd asked about Danny, but Sam had shrugged them off, saying he was a big boy and could take care of himself. The truth was that it was really getting to her that she didn't know where he was. She hadn't seen him since he'd disappeared from the benefit Saturday night.

Well, I'll be damned if I'm going to sit around this hotel room all day, Sam told herself firmly. *It's time for action.*

She pulled on her favorite worn jeans over a set of red men's long johns. She added her sheepskin vest and a red suede belt with three thongs that tied to create a tasseled effect. Stepping into her red cowboy boots, she spun to catch a glimpse of herself in the full-length mirror. "Serious vixen," she complimented herself out loud, and she was ready to attack the day.

One quick call to Wheels, the bike rental shop that Pres still managed, and she had arranged for a bicycle to be dropped off while she ate in the hotel's coffee shop. A bike was perfect for sleuthing around—it wasn't a black stallion with flaring nostrils, but what the hell.

An hour later she was braking outside the Bay View Motel's lobby just as the ferry shuttle—a worn-out old station wagon—dropped Kevin at the door.

Perfect timing, Sam congratulated herself. *A compadre!*

"Jeez," said Kevin with an ear-to-ear grin, "the welcome wagon never looked this good back where I come from!"

"Few people know I'm psychic," Sam said blithely. "I divined that you'd be arriving at this precise moment."

"It must be my lucky day," laughed Kevin. "So where does your psychic sense tell you Danny is?"

"Don't know," Sam confessed. "Your buddy has been making himself scarce of late."

Sam took Kevin to the motel, where he stopped to register and get a room key.

"Maybe we'll find him immersed in the great

American novel or something," Kevin said as they opened the door to the room he'd be sharing with Danny.

Sam was glad to see evidence that Danny hadn't disappeared into thin air: an open shaving kit, a damp towel on the shower rod, and a few shirts on hangers above a suitcase neatly stowed below.

A candidate for the Good Housekeeping award, thought Sam, picturing the helter-skelter disorder that had already blossomed in her room back at the hotel.

"Here's a note," said Kevin, handing her a scrap of motel notepaper.

Sam read aloud, "'Kev: Gone fishing. Back midmorning. Let's have lunch. D.'"

Sam's relief must have been evident. "You two having a spat or something?" Kevin asked.

"Whatever we're having, it isn't a good time," Sam replied testily. "Maybe if he'd show his face, we could figure out why."

As if on cue, the door opened and there was Danny.

"Hi, guys," said Danny, as casually as if he were just returning from a run across the street for a newspaper.

In spite of her resolution to stay cool, Sam was on her feet and in his face before he was three steps inside the room.

"Do you know how worried I've been?" she cried. "You could at least have left me a message or something!"

"Worried? Why?" said Danny. "This island is one of the safest places on earth."

"That's not what I mean," said Sam.

"So what do you mean?" Danny parried.

"Hey, time out, you two," Kevin interjected. "Sam, where'd you get that bike? Or more to the point, can I use it? I'll take a cruise and look at the island—not that the two of you aren't scintillating company right now," he added wryly.

"It's yours," Sam said. "Hey, I'm sorry, you just got here and—"

"Not to worry," Kevin interrupted. "I'll see you two later." He shut the door behind him.

Sam started in as soon as the door shut. "Listen, Danny, I—"

"No, you listen for a change," Danny said. "Somebody's got to start being honest around here, and I guess it's going to be me."

Sam waited. Danny paused for so long that she wasn't sure if he was going to talk or not. Finally he spoke, but as he did he stared down at his hands.

"Did I ever mention what a crappy childhood I had?" he asked Sam. "Yeah, yeah, yeah," he continued, "me and half of the Western world, right? Anyway, they didn't exactly send me off into the world with a lot of faith in relationships."

"I know the feeling," Sam said in a low voice.

"The point is that I've never wanted a . . . a relationship before," Danny said.

He looked up just as Sam was about to break in, but he stopped her. "Wait! I said I was going to be honest." His eyes locked on Sam and held her gaze. "The point is," he said slowly, "I've never *had* a relationship."

Sam wore a puzzled frown, and Danny paused until he saw the light dawn in her eyes.

"You mean . . ." Sam ventured, "you mean you're a . . ."

"That's right," said Danny.

Sam was astonished. Danny! Gorgeous, handsome, funny Danny, with the beautiful body and the bedroom eyes! Danny was a—

"That's not my only confession," Danny hurried on, as if he was afraid to lose momentum. "When I first met you, Sam, you were so outgoing, so cocky and sure of yourself. I thought you were the sexiest, and maybe one of the most experienced, girls I'd ever met."

"But Danny—" Sam began.

"Please, this is hard for me," Danny said painfully. "Don't you see? You talk so big, I figured you'd seduce me within a week. Then you'd go your way, and I'd go mine—a man of the world."

Sam was flabbergasted. All those nights, from wild partying to quiet talks, that she'd waited for Danny to try to kiss her. All this time, and he'd been waiting for *her* to make a move!

"There was only one problem," Danny continued. "I found out I really like you and I didn't want you to just go on your way."

Sam sat down on the bed. "Let me be sure I've got this straight. You were planning to let *me* take advantage of *you*?"

"Something like that," he agreed sheepishly.

She swung her hair back over her shoulder. "So then why haven't we done it yet?"

"Huh?" Danny said, taken aback.

Sam stood up. "Come on! Take off your clothes right now! Let's do it!"

"But—" Danny sputtered.

"You think you're so different from any other guy trying to get into my pants?" Sam yelled. "God, I should have known you weren't for real! I should have known never to trust you!"

"But nothing happened!" Danny protested. Now he was standing, too. "After you left Orlando, I started putting some of the pieces together about you. And you know what I figured out? You are totally full of it, Sam Bridges. You are all hot air."

"I am not!" Sam said furiously, her face turning red.

"You are!" Danny insisted, grabbing her arm. "You know the game and you've got the moves, but it's all a front. I bet you're no more experienced than I am. In love, or in anything else!"

Sam's heart thudded in her chest. "Oh yeah?" she asked with bravado.

"Yeah," Danny echoed softly.

An impasse.

"Well," Danny said finally. "Am I right?"

Sam felt tears quicken in her eyes. "I—"

"That's what I thought," Danny said softly, gently putting his arms around her.

194

"If you tell anyone, you're dead meat," Sam sniffled into his shoulder.

"Your secret is safe with me," Danny said.

When the knock came, Emma opened the suite door. No matter how often she saw Kurt, the sight of him always gave her a tingle. This evening, he looked especially handsome in the jacket and tie he had put on for their dinner date.

"Hiya, beautiful," Kurt said, stepping over the threshold to give her a quick, tantalizing kiss. "You look like every man's idea of a dream date."

Emma beamed with pleasure at the compliment. She was so thankful she'd thought to include one romantic evening dress in her packing—a white silk minishift whose simplicity belied its thousand-dollar price tag. Delicate bead work around the neck and cuffs was echoed in a pattern on her simple white kid-leather pumps.

Now she led Kurt into the suite, feeling sexy and feminine as the short skirt swished against her thighs.

"Would *monsieur* care for a glass of wine before dinner?" she asked over her shoulder, already making her way to the glass she was drinking herself. She'd had room service deliver a bottle of Pouilly-Fuissé so she could offer Kurt a drink before they went to dinner.

Something in Kurt's beautiful blue eyes changed. He gave her a studied look before saying, "Why don't we just go down to the restaurant?"

Oh, no, I've already managed to insult him,

Emma thought. Kurt had made it clear that he wished to pay for the entire evening, and she supposed he saw the Pouilly-Fuissé as something she had bought because he couldn't afford it.

"Good idea," Emma replied, finishing off the last of her wine. *Better just get out of here and on with the evening's plans*, she thought.

They were seated by the maître d' at one of the best tables in the inn's dining room, in a corner with windows on both sides offering views of the shoreline. Emma ordered veal Marsala, Kurt treated himself to a filet mignon, and they each had a glass of wine to complement their meals.

"I really missed you, Emma," Kurt told her. After dinner, he asked Emma if she'd like a cup of coffee.

"To be honest, I'd rather have a glass of champagne," she replied. She leaned closer and let the love shine in her eyes. "I feel like celebrating."

She'd hoped Kurt would see how much she appreciated his splurge for their dinner date, but his expression darkened ominously.

"Emma, I don't know how to say this except to just come right out with it," Kurt said solemnly. "It . . . well, it seems like you're drinking a lot."

Emma felt as though she'd been slapped.

"Really, Kurt," she managed tartly, "you make it sound like I've been tossing back shots of whiskey or something."

"Emma, tonight is Tuesday. You got here

Saturday, and every night since then, I've had to drive, because you weren't in any shape to get behind the wheel!"

"Well, if I'd known you minded driving—"

"I should add that it hasn't been very romantic having you fall asleep on my couch every night," Kurt continued. "I'm getting a little tired of throwing a blanket over you and knowing I'll have to deal with your headaches in the morning."

"I . . . it's only wine," Emma protested feebly.

"It's alcohol," Kurt said.

Something snapped in Emma. "Oh, please don't go getting self-righteous on me now!" she said.

"I'm not!" Kurt protested.

"Yes, you are," Emma said. "Why do you get to be the moral arbiter? You always do this!"

Kurt looked confused. "Hey, Em, come on, I don't—"

"You want to give me a sermon because I have an occasional glass of wine, but I bet if I said one word you'd have me in bed so fast I wouldn't know what hit me."

"Yes, I want to go to bed with you," Kurt said in a low, even voice. "That hasn't changed. But we've already agreed to take it slow. I'm not pushing for sex! I'd just like to be able to kiss you and . . . and be with you without you falling asleep because you've been drinking!"

"Well, thank you very much," Emma said frostily. "That's a delightful picture you've painted of me. But let me ask you this. If we've agreed to go slow, who is supposed to be the one putting on the brakes?"

Kurt just stared at her.

"Me, that's who," Emma said, answering her own question. She stood and dropped her napkin onto the table. "I'll be sleeping in my own room tonight. Thank you for a most enlightening evening."

With that, she turned and swept out of the dining room, leaving Kurt with his head in his hands.

THIRTEEN

It was Thursday before Carrie, Emma, and Sam managed a few hours together by themselves to have lunch and plan their party. They chose to meet at Crumpets, a new little tearoom that had just opened in preparation for the summer season.

After they'd ordered, Sam looked across the table at her two friends.

"Let's get right into the good stuff," she said mischievously. "I can't believe we've seen so little of each other. I've been going through withdrawal. Who's got a really hot story to tell?"

Neither Emma nor Carrie spoke immediately.

"No takers?" Sam asked innocently. "Well, then," she continued, "how about me?"

Emma and Carrie looked surprised.

"You mean you and Pres?" Emma asked.

"Not Pres," Sam said, wiggling her eyebrows.

"It's Danny!" Carrie broke in. "I knew it would be Danny eventually! All right!" she cheered.

"You mean you're . . ." Emma left the question unfinished.

"Yes!" Sam yelled. "I mean we're—"

"You slept with him?" Emma asked with a sharp intake of breath. Was she the only one who thought taking things slow was important? It just didn't seem like it would be the same unless she was sure she was in love.

"Wrong," Sam said. "Not yet. Not much of that stuff yet at all, actually," she admitted. "But he's a darned good kisser and we've agreed to, um, look at each other with lust."

"Good place to start!" Carrie agreed with a laugh.

"So how is Pres taking this?" Emma asked as the waitress brought them their chef's salads. "Actually, I haven't seen him around much."

"What's to take?" Sam asked with a shrug, pouring tons of thousand-island dressing on her salad. "Pres and I like to flirt with each other—it's never really been more than that. If you'll remember, the only reason we went out in the first place was to keep up with you lovebirds last summer."

"But you know what I don't understand?" Emma asked, nibbling daintily on a croissant. "We've asked you over and over about Danny, and you've always said you two were just friends."

Sam rolled her eyes. "Danny has this stupid idea that it's possible to be friends and be romantic at the same time. Personally, I think he's crazy," she said, reaching for her fork. "But you know me, the last of the great risk-takers."

"So how's the experiment going so far?" Carrie asked, sipping her water.

"I gotta tell you," Sam said with a huge grin, "I can't believe we waited this long to get to the hot part!"

"Before long I really will be the only virgin in the crowd," Emma said with a laugh.

"I'm not in any hurry," Sam informed them coolly.

Emma and Carrie stared at her.

"Excuse me, but is this the same Sam Bridges who was ready to do it with any good-looking stranger who caught her eye?" said Emma.

"That was then, this is now," Sam said dismissively.

"What's Danny have to say about that?" asked Carrie.

"It's okay with him," said Sam. She wasn't about to reveal his confession—that was just between the two of them.

She did feel almost ready to reveal something about herself, though. Sam had thought long and hard about it the night before. Danny was right. Lying to her best friends sucked. It was time to tell them she was no longer working at Disney World. But before she could open her mouth again, Carrie had focused on Emma.

"So are things blissful with you and Kurt?" Carrie asked.

"It's okay," Emma said quietly.

"Just okay?" Carrie prodded.

"We had a fight a couple nights ago, and I'm giving him some space."

Remembering Emma tottering out the door on Sunday, Sam wondered if the fight had been about her drinking.

"So what'd you fight about?" Sam ventured, reaching for another roll.

"It was just ridiculous," Emma sighed. She put down her fork and stared at her salad bowl. "He actually claimed I've been drinking too much wine lately."

Neither Carrie nor Sam said a word.

"I think what's really happening is that he isn't getting enough . . . attention from me. I think he wants me to sleep with him, and I'm just not ready for that."

"Well, Emma," Carrie said carefully, "I have noticed that you're drinking more than you used to."

"I have more problems than I used to," Emma snapped. She badly wanted to order a glass of wine right at that very moment, but willed herself not to. It would only add fuel to the fire.

"This salad was great," Sam said, forking up the last lettuce leaves, "but I'm still hungry." She grabbed the dessert menu and perused it. "So, Carrie, you must be the one with the hot inside info. What's going on with Billy?"

"He's been seeing someone else," Carrie said simply.

"Billy?" Sam asked in shock. "And he didn't even tell you?"

"He says he isn't sleeping with her," Carrie allowed, "and I believe him. I shut him out for a couple of days, and went off to shoot pictures, but he's been staying with me again, and it's been . . . almost perfect."

"Who is this girl?" asked Emma. "Does he intend to keep seeing her?"

"She actually seemed pretty cool," admitted Carrie. "I can see why he'd be attracted to her. She's sort of a world traveler, and right now she's a cook on one of those North Atlantic cruise ships. He met her when the Flirts played that weekend cruise back in March."

Sam was incredulous. "Hold on a sec. Am I picking up vibes that you've agreed to let him keep seeing her once you leave?"

"Sam, I don't have the right to let or not let him do something. He's a grownup. He makes his own choices."

"Hey, that's a little too New Age for me," Sam snorted. "If it were Danny, I'd deck him!"

"You're the biggest flirt in the Western hemisphere!" Carrie hooted. "Who are you to talk?"

"Flirting is permissible, for your information," Sam said coolly. "It's action that means war."

Carrie crumpled up her napkin and laid it by her plate. "I don't know what's going to happen. If he can last until June, at least we'll have the summer together. I've promised to be Graham and Claudia's au pair again."

"Yikes!" cried Sam. "I forgot to tell you what I did yesterday! Danny and Kevin rented a boat and went sailing, so I got a bike and rode around. I ended up going past the Jacobs place, and Dan was there! He's having a new roof put on and wanted to check the progress."

"Were the monsters along?" asked Carrie, referring to Dan's precocious thirteen-year-old identical-twin daughters.

"Only in spirit," said Sam. "The point is that he asked me back for the summer."

"And?" said Emma.

"And I told him I'd think about it."

"But what about Disney?" Carrie asked.

This was it. The big chance. The big opening. Truth time.

"I'm . . . having some problems at Disney," Sam ventured.

"Really?" Carrie asked, concern etched on her face.

"What is it?" Emma asked.

"It's . . . it's . . . oh, it's nothing," Sam said, brushing it off. She'd gotten so used to the lie, she just couldn't make herself tell them. She changed the subject quickly.

"Hey, listen, I picked up a magazine in the hotel lobby and there was an ad in there for dancers—dancers for an international touring company!" Sam said animatedly. "Would that be totally happening, or what?"

"Would that be long term?" Carrie asked. "You wouldn't be able to keep your job at Disney, would you?"

Sam sighed. "Honestly, Carrie. Didn't you ever hear of thinking big?"

Carrie looked a little hurt. "Well, how would you get in on it?"

"I have to send for more information," Sam replied. "I guess they have auditions. Just think—by next fall you two may be getting postcards from London, Paris—who knows?"

"Hi there!" came a low male voice.

The three girls looked up to see Kevin Logan standing at their table.

"Takeout," he said, holding up a bag of muffins. "How's it going?"

"Great!" said Sam. "We're about to move on to dessert."

"Try the Chocolate Sacrifice," Kevin suggested. "I had it yesterday. It's incredible." He glanced at each of them. "See you!"

Emma, Carrie, and Sam watched Kevin saunter out of the restaurant.

"Tell me that isn't a world-class butt," Sam murmured as they watched him walk out the door.

"You won't get any argument from me," Carrie said.

"Does he have a girlfriend, or what?" Emma asked casually.

"From what Danny tells me, he has a harem!" said Sam.

"Anyone for dessert?" the waitress asked cheerfully.

"Not me," said Emma.

"Or me," Carrie seconded quickly.

"Such wusses!" Sam chided. She turned to the waitress. "One Chocolate Sacrifice," she ordered, "and three spoons."

"So Kevin's a heartbreaker, is he?" Carrie said, immediately resuming their conversation.

"Not really a heartbreaker," Sam went on thoughtfully. "I think he just sort of plays the field, and he's so nice about it that girls feel lucky just to have his attention."

"He doesn't seem to have a big ego," Emma commented.

"He doesn't," Sam agreed. "There's something so solid about him—you know, he's smart, athletic, thoughtful, fun . . ."

"Maybe we should run him for president," Carrie offered.

The girls enjoyed a laugh, but Emma was thinking that she was glad Kevin was going to be around for the party. If Kurt was going to get on her case about her drinking, maybe she'd just spend time with Kevin. After all, he'd been really nice to her at her apartment. And he was very, very cute.

Emma sighed and stared into the distance. Love was not all it was cracked up to be. Not at all.

By seven-thirty Saturday evening, the party plans had materialized. The Templetons' house was lit up like a Christmas tree, with munchies set around in each room and a buffet table loaded

206

with goodies. Emma had sprung for trays of the Bay View Café's famous fried chicken, and Sam and Carrie had spent hours on fresh-vegetable dips and homemade biscuits. The Flirts had contributed a keg of beer, which was chilling in a tub of ice on the deck, and the girls had stashed extra bags of ice in the freezer, knowing that some people would bring their own liquor for mixed drinks.

As usual, the three girls couldn't have chosen three more different outfits. Carrie had on her new raspberry jacket again, but this time she wore a sexy black bodysuit and black jeans underneath. She'd spent an hour putting the outfit on and then taking it off again, trying to decide if she looked fat. Finally, she'd simply forced herself to decide.

Emma had on a short pleated skirt in pink-and-purple plaid, with a long pink cashmere sweater that slipped sexily off one shoulder. Sam had chosen a lime-green bodysuit, and paired it with a wide belt covered in Mickey Mouse stickers and an oversized man's jacket from the Salvation Army.

"I can't believe our week is almost over—it went so fast!" Carrie exclaimed wistfully as she ladled out one more bowl of salsa. "I'll be back in the dorm study room wondering if it ever happened at all!" *Still sticking my finger down my throat*, she added in her head. *Still desperate to find another way.* She missed the feeling of being able to talk to Sam and Emma about anything.

"And I'll be back reading nineteenth-century French literature at Goucher College," Emma said, wrinkling her nose. *And not getting up the courage to change my life. Drinking it away.*

I don't even know where I'll be was Sam's scary thought. *One thing I vow, though, is that I will not go back to Junction!* She had promised Danny that she'd go back to Orlando with him. But after that, life was a blur. There was always the chance she could get back on at Big Al's, and maybe that ad for the international dance tour would pan out.

"But I refuse to think about it now!" Sam said aloud to no one in particular. She cranked up the tunes and did a little boogie across the living room. "Let's party!"

The front door opened, and the first guest arrived. To everyone's surprise, it was Daphne, carrying a platter of brownies.

"Hi," Daphne said shyly, meeting the girls' gazes one by one. "I brought something to donate to the party."

Carrie was the first to rush up. "You didn't have to," she said with a smile. "But yum—we're glad you did! Come on in, and let's find room for these on the main table."

No sooner had they walked around the corner than the door opened again to let Flash Hathaway slither in.

"Right on the heels of every silver lining, there's a big ugly cloud," cracked Sam.

"How can he have the nerve to show his slimy

face on this island after everything he's done?" Emma asked in shock.

"Hiya, chicks," said Flash, oblivious to Sam's slam. "Got any food around here? I got an engagement party to snap on the other side of the island, and thought I'd drop in for dinner first." Helping himself to a chip with salsa, Flash continued as he chewed, "Where's the third Mouseketeer? Or is she so intimidated by a professional photographer that she ran when she saw me coming?"

"Would you like a napkin?" asked Emma as Flash noisily licked his fingertips, then plunged back in for another chip.

"How about a bib?" said Sam with distaste.

Ignoring Sam, Flash said to Emma, "Sure, Blondie, I'll take a napkin. Let's go in here where the real eats are, and you can tie it on for me."

At that moment, Kevin and Danny walked through the door, Danny going straight to Sam for a hug. Kevin greeted Emma with an exaggerated bow and a kiss for her hand.

"I see the royal family's arrived," said Flash, giving Emma a nod as he moved toward the buffet in the dining room. "Excuse me, Princess Di."

"Oh well," said Sam, following his exit with her gaze, "it's not really a party without at least one slob in the crowd."

Kevin offered to help Emma uncork wine bottles, and Danny and Sam iced the soft drinks he'd brought. Sam found herself hoping that Emma wouldn't drink too much, but the thought put a damper on her party mood. *What the hell*, she told herself, *it's a party—let everyone do what they want.* She decided on the spot to have a beer herself.

Carrie and Daphne were touring the Templetons' house, and Carrie found herself desperately wanting to ask Daphne about her eating disorder. Maybe here was someone who would understand. She chose the balcony off the master bedroom to pose her question.

"I don't mean to pry," Carrie explained, "but I'm kind of curious about what you went through. I mean, your recovery. See, I have this . . . friend . . ."

A shrewd and searching look came into Daphne's eyes but was gone a second later. "Well, there are different kinds of eating disorders. I thought I couldn't eat at all, which is usually called anorexia. But it's complicated. Some people can eat, but then they make themselves throw up afterward, and that's called bulimia."

"Yes, I've . . . I've heard of it," Carrie said. "That's what my friend has."

"Well, your friend is probably really unhappy," Daphne said. "It's really painful."

Carrie felt like someone had hit her in her stomach with a fist. Yes, it really *was* painful! How could it have possibly happened to her? To *her?*

"Anyway, at least your friend has taken the right first step," Daphne said.

"What's that?" Carrie asked.

"She told you! After that, it's her call. There are entire books on the subject! People have all kinds of ways they recover: reading, counseling, groups, programs."

"Oh, well, she's not the kind of person to join a program or something," Carrie said hastily. "I don't think she's been doing it for very long or anything."

Daphne looked at her thoughtfully. "Well, maybe she'll surprise herself. I sure surprised myself."

They were interrupted by a couple who claimed they were also just touring the house, though Carrie suspected they were probably scoping out bedrooms in case the party got "private" later. Suddenly Carrie felt responsible for the Templetons' house, and ushered Daphne back toward the hub of activity downstairs.

"Gosh, just when I thought there were no good-looking girls at this party!" It was Billy, first leaning over her shoulder, then pulling her close for a hug.

Please let things work out this summer, prayed Carrie. *I love him so much!* The week of honesty with Billy had given her the courage to tell Josh she had made her decision. She would just have to take her chances. Maybe Josh would find a girlfriend who would tolerate Carrie's friendship with him, and they could still be friends. Very briefly, Sarah Lovett popped into her mind. She wondered if that was who Josh had in mind. She also wondered if she should have a chat with

Sarah about bulimia. *There I go again*, she thought. *Fair-and-square Carrie.*

"I brought some rum," said Billy. "Want a Sunset Mambo?"

Carrie hardly ever drank—she didn't particularly care for it. But tonight she felt like celebrating with Billy. "Sure," she answered. "Just be sure to make it a light one."

"Don't worry about that." Billy laughed, and Carrie knew he was thinking of the night the summer before when she had tried to impress him with her drinking, and ended up being sick as a dog. She laughed, too, and they made their way to the kitchen.

Emma was holding court near the counter where the wine was set out. With Kurt on one side and Kevin on the other, she was feeling charming and uninhibited. Both guys were extremely attractive, but Emma knew it was Kurt who had claim to her heart. They were even getting along better than they had all week. In honor of the party, she supposed, he wasn't giving her any trouble about drinking, and had even refilled her glass for her.

Kevin was telling a funny story, and suddenly Emma wished she had a picture of the three of them laughing and talking together. With her all-girls private-schooling education, she had never had the chance to know boys as friends. Now she realized that the attraction she felt for Kevin had to do with his being such a likeable person.

212

"The guy actually expected me to talk to this turtle," said Kevin, finishing the story about his first interview assignment.

Emma watched Kurt laughing and thought, *I'm happy just being near him!* The wineglass she was turning in her hand drew her momentarily into thoughts of their quarrel. *He's right,* she thought, *I need to think about this—but not tonight.*

Sam, too, was having a grand time. Slightly buzzed from the beer she'd been drinking, she had taken over the job of DJ. Since everyone else seemed even less sober, no one minded giving her the job, and she played one dance tune after another: funky blues, hard rock, Motown, and even a Broadway number or two, just to keep the crowd on their toes.

Danny watched with amusement as she tried to get the crowd to follow a Disney dance routine. He was the only one in the room who could appreciate her exact impersonation of Mr. Christopher, and she felt a strong, warm connection flowing between them. She ran back to the stereo and chose a slow dance, so she could enjoy the rhythm of their bodies moving together in time to the music. Funny, the change in their relationship didn't feel strange to her at all. She could tell he didn't even mind when she roped Pres into being her partner for the twist a couple of numbers later.

By midnight, everyone was dancing, and an hour later, Carrie noticed that there were beginning to be casualties. She rallied her fellow hostesses to start winding things down before they ended up with an all-night party on their hands. Sam was resistant at first, but reluctantly put on an album of ballads, and helped assess the damages.

A few guests were lolling in armchairs, and had to be helped to their feet and walked to the door. Someone had broken a beer bottle in one of the bathrooms, and someone else had thrown up in the shower stall of another. Upstairs, Kurt and Danny found a couple in the guest room who had undressed and gone to bed as if they were home. Emma found an unidentified brassiere flying like a flag from the edge of the deck.

"I'd say we had some fun," Sam announced as she cleaned a salsa spill from the hardwood floor in the dining room. "But how did we end up drunking so mich?"

Her remark drew a laugh from the last few stragglers who were still on their feet; most had congregated at the buffet for a final munch. Now they wandered off to find shoes, purses, and jackets for the trek home.

Carrie had marshaled Kevin and Billy into a crew to sweep through the outlying areas of the house for used cups and empty bottles. They returned as she was running a sinkful of soapy water to start washing a few of the serving dishes.

"What's this, the party's over?" Kevin ribbed

her. "Hey, don't clean up now. We can come back and help with this tomorrow."

"I think you mean later today," yawned Carrie. "It must be four in the morning or something. Anyway, I'd like to get started on it tonight, but I'm not sure I can stay awake."

"What you need is some fresh air," Kevin claimed, grabbing her by the waist and waltzing her toward the door. "I hereby, forthwith—and also right now—proclaim a beach walk!" he went on to announce in a booming, comical voice.

"Yes!" cried Emma as the idea grabbed her imagination. "Throw caution to the wind! It's almost our last night on the island! Let's do it. We can watch the sunrise!"

"I'm in!" Sam decided.

"Sounds like fun to me," said Danny.

"Only one problem," Kurt pointed out. "No beach."

For some reason, that struck everyone as being hilarious. No beach! Maybe they were just a *little* drunk . . .

"What do you mean? We're surrounded by beaches!" Billy exclaimed. "It's just a question of getting to one."

"We can use my car," offered Emma, "but I'm not sure we can all fit. Unless . . ."

Like a chorus being directed by a single hand, the cry went up in unison: "Unless we put the top down!"

It took only a minute to decide it was a great idea.

Grabbing up whatever they could find in the way of warm clothing, they tumbled out the door and into the driveway. Emma was weaving as she tried to fit the key in the lock.

"One requirement," said Kevin, coming up behind Emma. He placed a hand over hers and gently extracted her keys. "I drive. Friends don't let friends, and all that."

"Man, are you sure you're okay?" asked Billy. "I'd offer myself, but I'm honestly a little polluted."

"No problem," said Kevin, opening the door and sliding in behind the wheel.

It seemed pointless to argue, and in fact, though Kevin had been drinking with them all night, he seemed able to hold his liquor without much effect. In a minute, the top was whirring smoothly into its bed. Kurt grabbed Emma around the waist and pulled her onto his lap in the passenger seat. Laughing and stumbling against each other, the rest of the group scrambled for space in the back seat of the open car. A rock station blared out "Twist and Shout," and everyone sang along at the top of their lungs.

"This is living!" Sam hollered over the noise, throwing her arms up to the night sky.

The Beatles song ended and an old Johnny Mathis ballad came on.

"Boring!" Kevin called out as he took the first turn onto the narrow road that led to the beach.

"Find some rap!" Sam yelled from the back seat.

"Rap? Yuck!" Danny put in from next to her. "Find some good rock!"

"He likes the Grateful Dead!" Sam teased.

"Wow! Huggie-Veggie!" Billy teased him.

"You like the Grateful Dead, too!" Carrie laughed, hitting Billy in the arm.

Sam leaned into Danny impulsively and gave him a kiss on the lips.

"Driver's choice!" Emma called into the wind. "You pick, Kevin!"

A number of things happened very fast just then. "Let me see," yelled Sam, lunging forward to reach for the tape Kurt had pulled out of the glove compartment. Kevin swatted playfully at Sam's hand, and a pair of headlights appeared directly in front of them, seemingly out of nowhere.

"Hang on!" yelled Kevin.

Danny and Billy both reached forward in a vain attempt to take control as Kevin lost his grip on the wheel.

Brakes squealed from every direction. The car seemed to whirl off into space, and the sky exploded.

Although Sam and Danny would later say they remembered lying in the woods and looking up to see the car bent around a tree, no one else remembered much of anything until the ambulance arrived. Even then, what they remembered were pulsing red lights and strange faces looking down at them with the bare tree branches surrounding their heads like crowns of thorns.

What all of them would remember with brilliant clarity for the rest of their lives was the moment in the emergency room's waiting area, where a group of nurses and doctors were helping them fill out forms and preparing to treat the most serious injuries first. They were all suffering from some degree of shock, and the room was already strangely quiet when a tall doctor with wire-rimmed glasses gave them the inconceivable news that Kevin was dead.

FOURTEEN

Sunday morning was bright and clear, and so cold that the wind seemed to be singing in the ears of the small crowd at the ferry dock. An eerie unreality cloaked the group, as if this sunny day were something in their imaginations—a movie, maybe.

Please let the screen go dark and the house lights come up, and let us all walk out of here laughing, prayed Sam. But minute to minute, the story kept right on unfolding, leaving the hapless actors to play it out without the helping hand of writer, director, or editor to change the ending.

They were gathered to watch the ferry leave with Kevin's body. Kevin's body. No one could grasp the full meaning.

Danny was going, too, to meet Kevin's parents on the other side. The Logans didn't want to cross the other way and see the island where their young son had died so unexpectedly.

Ken Miner, owner of the Play Café, had been a godsend. He hadn't known Kevin well, but he was old enough to have dealt with death before. Billy, not knowing who else to call, had phoned Ken from the hospital, and Ken had come right over.

Somehow calls had been made and plans set into motion, with Ken taking charge. The hospital staff had handled the group from the car accident with professional kindness, patching up injuries where they could and acknowledging the grief and shock that follows sudden loss.

Emma had suffered a broken collarbone and a dislocated shoulder. One of Carrie's ears had been partially torn off where her head had scraped a tree as she flew from the car. The skilled hands of the staff surgeon had set Emma's bones and stitched Carrie's ear, and the girls were assured of complete recovery after a reasonable amount of mending time.

Sam and Danny, tumbling from the side of the car that had leaned into the woods, hadn't had far to fall and had cushioned each other's roll down the embankment. Danny's nose had been bloodied but not broken, and Sam had a patchwork of scrapes and bruises along her arms and legs.

Billy had landed outside the car on his right hand, which had been fractured in several places. Since he used his guitar mostly for songwriting, his injury didn't threaten his livelihood, and the prescribed future sessions of physical therapy didn't seem a high price to pay for walking away with only a small cast.

Kurt, however, had appeared to be in critical

condition when the ambulance had first arrived. He had been propelled straight into the edge of the windshield, leaving him unconscious and with an angry gash in his forehead. But his eyelids had fluttered as the ambulance reached the emergency entrance, and by the time he was wheeled through the doors on a gurney he was able to speak.

"Lucky he didn't break his neck," Sam had overheard one of the policemen remark to an orderly. "I tell my kids again and again that I've yet to unstrap a dead body from a seat belt. I just hope they're listening better than these kids here—it's a crying shame."

Now, watching the ferry pull away from its moorings and churn off into the sea, the living people left on the dock shared a question that they each sent out to their respective gods: *Why? Why Kevin, and not us?*

"Life is really extremely fragile," the kindly doctor had told them as they had left the hospital before dawn. His brows were knit together in earnest sadness, as if he could somehow get something across to these kids that they couldn't possibly know at such young ages. "There's so much we don't know. I wish I could tell you I had answers. . . ."

But he didn't. No one did. All anyone had was theories. And the group on the dock, most of them sobbing openly, could not take much comfort today in the idea of a higher power.

"Not much point in standing here," said Ken,

opening his arms to them all in a gesture of inclusion. "Let's get back to the house. Work is good therapy, and there's a cleanup to do today."

The house, Claudia and Graham's, had been their retreat a few hours ago after the hospital staff had herded them gently toward the door. Obviously they couldn't stay at the hospital, but no one wanted to leave, as if staying there could suspend them forever in a limbo where Kevin might suddenly reappear. Ken had taken them all back to the Templetons', since the thought of being alone was unbearable to any of them.

Now, seated (and belted) in stunned silence in Ken's car, they were headed back to begin facing reality. Looking out the car window, Carrie found her thoughts repeating like a needle on a scratched record. In her head, she saw a huge clock face, its hands turning backward, and she thought that maybe if she concentrated hard enough, she could make it happen. *If only it were yesterday! I'd call off the party. I'd hide Emma's car keys. I'd do the dishes and make everyone help me. I'd . . .*

As if a magnet were pulling them, Carrie's eyes turned with everyone else's as they passed the spot where they'd crashed.

No one wanted to look at the tree, but everybody found their eyes riveted to that side of the road. The car, of course, had been removed and towed somewhere by the police. But splintered bark and the fresh white wound on the tree's trunk offered visible proof that the nightmare really had happened.

Emma foraged through her thoughts for a shred of the past that would seem meaningful. All of it—her childhood, her years at Aubergame, her months at Goucher, her parents' quarrels, her mother with Austin Payne, her father with Valerie, her new car—it all seemed cluttered with the most trivial of details. What, exactly, were the crushing problems that had made her so miserable lately?

In trying to comprehend Kevin's death, a terrible truth was descending on her. *This is life,* she realized. *This is why people say it's hard.* She thought of her griping, her self-pity, her drinking—had those times really been so difficult? Compared to how she felt now, her previous troubles seemed silly and indulgent. She almost started crying again when she remembered how cool she had thought she would look in her expensive new car. *How foolish I was! Just look where that got us. Just look where it got Kevin.*

Ken let them out in the driveway. "I have to get over to the café for a few hours—I'm taking estimates on the finish work today. I'll call later to see if there's anything you need." He seemed to have more to say, but in the end let it go at that, and backed around carefully before rolling out of the drive.

Huddling uncertainly in the midmorning sun, Carrie, Sam, Emma, Kurt, and Billy observed the house and the front door they'd have to find the strength to enter once more. For a moment, no one moved or spoke. Then Kurt's voice broke the silence.

"Please, everybody." Kurt's words came choking out. "Please tell me if I'm crazy—is anyone else standing here hoping that we'll open the door and find Kevin telling stories in there?"

"Oh Kurt!" Sam cried, her voice breaking into a sob as she spoke for all of them. "You're not crazy."

With arms linked, the five friends moved together to start back into the world of the living.

Somehow the hours passed. Furniture was put back in place, dishes were washed, rugs were vacuumed, counters wiped, and trash hauled out. Everyone was amazed—and sickened—by the sheer volume of bottles, cans, and glasses. The thought of how much they'd had to drink the night before horrified them.

"People say it's stupid to feel guilty," Carrie sniffled. "How else are we supposed to feel?"

"I think this is pretty unfair punishment, just for having fun," Sam added shakily.

"We had way too much to drink last night," sobbed Emma, "and I'm as guilty as anyone. Wherever he is now, Kevin has every right to hate us."

"Hold it, guys," Kurt interjected, barely holding his own tears back. "I haven't really got a grip on this yet, but I do know one thing. Kevin had as much fun as anyone last night. I don't know where he is, but I do know he doesn't hate us!"

"I don't know," Billy said, trying to keep his lip from trembling. "We really screwed up."

Suddenly Sam felt angry. "Kevin was drinking, too—why did he say he could drive?"

"Why did we let him?" mourned Emma, feeling especially awful since she would have been at the wheel if she hadn't had so much to drink. *If I hadn't been drowning my pitiful sorrows in a bottle of wine all week*, she added to herself.

But Sam wasn't finished. "It was his damned idea to go to the beach in the first place!" she cried, winding into a fury. Suddenly snatching a throw pillow from the couch, she held it at eye level and shook it violently. "Damn you, Kevin Logan! You jerk! You fool! You butthead! You, you—" Sam threw the pillow and dissolved into tears.

Kurt and Billy left at about two in the afternoon because the girls said they wanted to be alone for a while.

"Are you sure?" Kurt asked Emma. "I'll stay with you," he offered.

"Thanks," she said, smiling tremulously. "I . . . I'm not sure what I want. But I need to be with Sam and Carrie for a little while."

He hugged her fiercely. Billy hugged Carrie, and then they left.

Now that they were alone, the girls couldn't really find anything to say to one another. Words seemed . . . silly. Pointless. Nothing seemed to have any meaning. So they sat in the living room, staring out the picture window as the afternoon wore on, trying to understand.

As the room began to grow darker Emma found her voice. "Do you think it's some kind of lesson from God?" she asked in a tiny voice.

"I don't believe in God," Sam said bitterly.

"Sam!" Carrie said in shock.

"I don't!" Sam repeated viciously. "You think a great guy like God's supposed to be would let Kevin die like this?"

"Maybe there's some kind of . . . force, some kind of plan," Emma said.

"I think it's all just random violence," Sam said bitterly.

"I couldn't cope if I didn't believe in God," Carrie said earnestly.

"So tell me how this God justifies taking Kevin's life, then?" Sam asked shrilly. "I'd really like to know."

No one had an answer.

"It makes me feel . . . ashamed," Emma finally said in a hushed voice.

"It sure puts things into perspective," Carrie said, hugging her knees up to her chest.

"That's what I mean," Emma continued earnestly. "I was thinking about my drinking. You two tried to tell me, Kurt tried . . . and it's such crap, isn't it? All that 'poor me' stuff that I use as an excuse to drink. But I'm alive! I'm alive!"

Tears came to Carrie's eyes. "I was a terrible friend to you, Em. Because I saw how much you were drinking, and I didn't really say anything much."

"I guess I thought you'd all think less of me if I really admitted I had a problem," Emma said.

"I . . . I have a problem, too," Carrie managed in a tiny voice. She gulped and took a deep breath. "This is so hard. Okay, here goes. I . . . I think I have an eating disorder."

Sam raised herself on one elbow from where she'd been flopped on the couch. "You? An eating disorder? Don't be silly!"

"What do you mean, Carrie?" asked Emma.

For what felt like the thousandth time that day, Carrie's eyes swam with tears. "I was having these terrible fights with Josh, and working real hard, and studying late, and worrying about money and my grades. So I started eating to feel better, then I gained weight and felt worse than ever! It seemed like my whole life was totally out of control."

"I know how that feels," Emma said wryly.

"Anyway," Carrie went on, "this girl in my dorm was throwing up after meals to keep her weight down, and one night I caught her." Carrie turned to Sam. "Just like you caught me the other night at Emma's apartment. Only I couldn't tell you the truth."

"You mean you make yourself—" Sam mimed putting her finger down her throat.

Carrie hung her head and nodded.

"Poor baby!" said Sam. She rushed over to Carrie and hugged her. "Why didn't you tell us?"

"I'm so ashamed," Carrie sobbed. "And I don't think I even know how to stop now!"

Emma sat down on the other side of Carrie and without thinking she put her arms around her, holding her and rocking her in a way that strangely comforted her at the same time.

"Carrie, you're so strong and smart and talented," Emma crooned. "You'll handle this!"

"But that's just it!" Carrie sobbed. "I always handle everything. I don't think I can handle one more thing!"

"You can do it," Sam assured her. "You need to get some help, though, like from the counseling service at Yale."

Emma pushed her bangs out of her face and tried to smile. "It seems terrible, doesn't it, that it takes some tragedy to make us face our problems?"

"It's just not fair," Sam said passionately. "But at least we've got a shot at it. Kevin doesn't."

"Let's not waste it!" Carrie said fervently.

Emma looked at her friends. "I've been an idiot. I was so afraid you'd judge me."

"I've been an idiot, too," Carrie said. "I wanted to tell you both so much, but I was afraid."

"Good thing for you two that I'm the model of mental health," Sam said. She waited a moment. "God, am I full of it. Even now, I'm so used to lying that I can hardly tell the truth."

"About what?" Emma asked with surprise.

"About my job, or my lack of job," Sam blurted out. "I got fired."

"You what?" Carrie asked.

"Fired," Sam repeated. "As in no job. As in unemployed. The choreographer said I was too original."

"So why didn't you just tell us?" Emma asked with surprise.

"Oh, sure," Sam said, getting up from the couch. "You two in college, everything just hunky-dory, and me, the dropout, I can't even hold down a job."

"Well, everything isn't hunky-dory," Carrie said. "And we would have understood."

"Maybe," Sam allowed grudgingly.

"And maybe we've been underestimating one another," Emma said quietly. She went to the window and looked out toward the road, the road where everything had changed.

No one said a word for a moment.

"I'm a better person than this," Emma finally whispered softly.

"You're a wonderful person," Sam agreed.

Emma turned to her, her eyes bright with tears. "So are you. And you!" she said, turning to Carrie.

Carrie hugged the pillow to herself. "We can't bring him back, and I don't know what it all means," she said, her eyes shining. "I do know this: that the only thing we can do to make Kevin's death meaningful, is to try to live the very best lives we can."

"But it won't change a thing!" Sam cried angrily. "He'll still be dead. And we'll still feel like we screwed up for having let him drive after we knew he'd been drinking."

"Sam's right," Emma agreed.

"Maybe there's a bigger plan, and we just can't see it," Carrie whispered.

"I'd like to believe that," Emma said softly.

"I'd like to believe in *something*," Sam said in a choked voice, tears rolling down her cheeks.

"Well, we'll have to start with ourselves, and work up from there," Carrie said. "And just think, in only two months we'll all be here together again. And then we can look out for each other."

"And no more secrets," Emma added.

Carrie and Sam nodded. The three girls stared out over the bay, watching the sun disappear below the horizon.

ABOUT THE AUTHOR

In addition to writing novels for young adults, Cherie Bennett is an award-winning playwright, an actress, and a singer. Cherie lives in Nashville, Tennessee.

*Sam, Carrie, and Emma return to Sunset Island and their summer jobs as au pairs...
Let the adventure begin!*

By Cherie Bennett

___*SUNSET HEAT* #7 (June 1992)   0-425-13383-4/$3.50**

Sam is hired by a talent scout to dance in a show in Japan. Unfortunately, Emma and Carrie don't share her enthusiasm. No one really knows if this is on the up and up, especially after her fiasco with the shifty photographer last summer. But Sam is determined to go despite her friends. . .

___*SUNSET PROMISES* #8 (July 1992)   0-425-13384-2/$3.50**

Carrie receives a lot of attention when she shows her photos at the Sunset Gallery. She is approached by a publisher who wants her to do a book of pictures of the island. But when Carrie photos the entire island, she discovers a part of Sunset Island that tourists never see...

___*SUNSET SCANDAL* #9 (August 1992)   0-425-13385-0/$3.50**

Emma has started to see Kurt again, and everything's going great...until Kurt is arrested as the suspect in a rash of robberies! He has no alibi, and things look pretty bad. Then, Emma befriends a new girl on the island who might be able to help prove Kurt's innocence.

___*SUNSET WHISPERS* #10 (September 1992)   0-425-13386-9/$3.50**

Sam is shocked to find out she is adopted. She's never needed her friends more than when her birth mother comes to Sunset Island to meet her. And to add to the chaos, Sam and Emma, along with the rest of the girls on the island, are auditioning to be back up in the rock band *Flirting with Danger*.
